**It didn't matter that the hamburger joint was littered with uniformed police officers. Mia knew it was him the moment he walked in the door.**

Officer Collin Grace sure stood out in a crowd. Brown eyes full of caution swept the room once, as if calculating escape routes, before coming to rest on her. She prided herself on being able to read people. Officer Collin Grace didn't trust a soul in the place.

Mia fixed her attention on the policeman. With spiked dark hair, slashing eyebrows, and a five-o'clock shadow, he was good-looking in a hard, manly kind of way.

He came over and jacked up an eyebrow. "Miss Carano?"

A bewildering flutter tickled her stomach. "Yes, but I prefer Mia."

He slid into the booth, and didn't ask her to use his given name. She wasn't surprised. He was every bit the cool, detached cop. This wasn't going to be easy.

**Books by Linda Goodnight**

Love Inspired

*In the Spirit of...Christmas* #326
*A Very Special Delivery* #349
**A Season for Grace* #377

**The Brothers' Bond*

## *LINDA GOODNIGHT*

A romantic at heart, Linda Goodnight believes in the traditional values of family and home. Writing books enables her to share her certainty that, with faith and perseverance, love can last forever and happy endings really are possible.

A native of Oklahoma, Linda lives in the country with her husband, Gene, and Mugsy, an adorably obnoxious rat terrier. She and Gene have a blended family of six grown children. An elementary school teacher, she is also a licensed nurse. When time permits, Linda loves to read, watch football and rodeo, and indulge in chocolate. She also enjoys taking long, calorie-burning walks in the nearby woods. Readers can write to her at linda@lindagoodnight.com, or c/o Steeple Hill Books, 233 Broadway, Suite 1001, New York, NY 10279.

# A Season for Grace

Linda Goodnight

Published by Steeple Hill Books™

STEEPLE HILL BOOKS

ISBN-13: 978-0-373-87411-8
ISBN-10: 0-373-87411-1

A SEASON FOR GRACE



All characters in this book have no existence outside the imagination of the author and have no relation whatsoever to anyone bearing the same name or names. They are not even distantly inspired by any individual known or unknown to the author, and all incidents are pure invention.

This edition published by arrangement with Steeple Hill Books.



www.SteepleHill.com

**Printed in U.S.A.**

A father to the fatherless, defender of widows,
is God in his holy dwelling. God sets
the lonely in families.

—*Psalms* 68:5–6

Special thanks to former DHS caseworker Tammy Potter for answering my social services questions, and to my buddy Maggie Price for helping me keep my cop in the realm of reality. Any mistakes or literary license are my own. I would also like to acknowledge the legion of foster and adoptive parents and children who have shared their insight into the painful world of social orphans.

# *Prologue*

The worst was happening again. And there was nothing he could do about it.

Collin Grace was only ten years old but he'd seen it all and then some. One thing he'd seen too much of was social workers. He hated them. The sweet-talking women with their briefcases and straight skirts and fancy fingernails. They always meant trouble.

Arms stiff, he stood in front of the school counselor's desk and stared at the office wall. His insides shook so hard he thought he might puke. But he wouldn't ask to be excused. No way he'd let them know how scared he was. Wouldn't do no good anyhow.

Betrayal, painful as a stick in the eye, settled low in his belly. He had thought Mr. James liked him, but the counselor had called the social worker.

Didn't matter. Collin wasn't going to cry. Not like

his brother Drew. Stupid kid was fighting and kicking and screaming like he could stop what was happening.

"Now, Drew." The social worker tried to soothe the wild brother. Tried to brush his too-long, dark hair out of his furious blue eyes. Drew snarled like a wounded wolf. "Settle down. Everything will be all right."

That was a lie. And all three of the brothers knew it. Nothing was ever all right. They'd leave this school and go into foster care again. New people to live with, new school, new town, all of them strange and unfriendly. They'd be cleaned up and fattened up, but after a few months Mama would get them back. Then they'd be living under bridges or with some drugged-out old guy who liked to party with Mama. Then she'd disappear. Collin would take charge. Things would be better for a while. The whole mess would start all over again.

People should just leave them alone. He could take care of his brothers.

Drew howled again and slammed his seven-year-old fist into the social worker. "I hate you. Leave me alone!"

He broke for the door.

Collin bit the inside of his lip. Drew hadn't figured out yet that he couldn't escape.

A ruckus broke out. The athletic counselor grabbed Drew and held him down in a chair even though he bucked and spat and growled like a mad tomcat. Drew was a wiry little twerp; Collin gave him credit for that. And he had guts. For what good it would do him, he might as well save his energy. Grown-ups would win. They always did.

People passed the partially open office door and peered around the edge, curious about all the commotion. Collin tried to pretend he couldn't see them, couldn't hear them. But he could.

"Poor little things," one of the teachers murmured. "Living in a burned-out trailer all by themselves. No wonder they're filthy."

Collin swallowed the cry of humiliation rising up in his stomach like the bad oranges he'd eaten from the convenience-store trash. He did the best he could to keep Drew and Ian clean and fed. It wasn't easy without water or electricity. He'd tried washing them off in the restroom before school, but he guessed he hadn't done too good a job.

"Collin." The fancy-looking social worker had a hand on her stomach where Drew had punched her. "You've been through this before. You know it's for the best. Why don't you help me get your brothers in the car?"

Collin didn't look at her. Instead he focused on his brothers, sick that he couldn't help them. Sick with dread. Who knew what would happen this time? Somehow he had to find a way to keep them all together. That was the important thing. Together, they could survive.

Ian, only four, looked so little sitting in a big brown plastic chair against the wall. His scrawny legs stuck straight out and the oversized tennis shoes threatened to fall off. No shoestrings. They stunk, too. Collin could smell them clean over here.

Like Collin, baby Ian didn't say a word; he didn't fight. He just cried. Silent, broken tears streamed down his cheeks and left tracks like a bicycle through mud. Clad in a plaid flannel shirt with only two buttons and a pair of Drew's tattered jeans pulled together at the belt loops with a piece of electrical cord, his skinny body trembled. Collin could hardly stand that.

They shouldn't have come to school today; then none of this would have happened. But they were hungry and he was fresh out of places to look. School lunch was free, all you could eat.

Seething against an injustice he couldn't name or defend against, he crossed the room to his brother. He didn't say a word; just put his hand on Ian's head. The little one, quivering like a scared puppy, relaxed the tiniest bit. He looked up, eyes saying he trusted his big brother to take care of everything the way he always did.

Collin hoped he could.

The social worker knelt in front of Ian and took his hand. "I know you're scared, honey, but you're going to be fine. You'll have plenty to eat and a nice, safe place to sleep." She tapped his tennis shoes. "And a new pair of shoes, just your size. Things will be better, I promise."

Ian sniffed and dragged a buttonless sleeve across his nose. When he looked at her, he had hope in his eyes. Poor little kid.

Collin ignored the hype. He'd heard it all before and it was a lie. Things were never better. Different, but not better.

The tall counselor, still holding Drew in the chair, slid to his knees just like the social worker and said, "Boys, sometimes life throws us a curveball. But no matter what happens, I want you to remember one thing. Jesus cares about you. If you let him, He'll take care of you. No matter where you go from here, God will never walk off and leave you."

A funny thing happened then. Drew sort of quieted down and looked as if he was listening. Ian was still sniffin' and snubbin', but watching Mr. James, too. None of them could imagine *anybody* who wouldn't leave them at some point.

"Collin?" The counselor, who Collin used to like a lot, twisted around and stretched an open palm toward him. Collin wanted to take hold. But he couldn't.

After a minute, Mr. James dropped his hand, laid it on Collin's shoe. Something about that big, strong hand on his old tennis shoe bothered Collin. He didn't know if he liked it or hated it.

The room got real quiet then. Too quiet. Mr. James bowed his bald head and whispered something. A prayer, Collin thought, though he didn't know much about such things. He stared at the wall, trying hard not to listen. He didn't dare hope, but the counselor's words made him want to.

Then Mr. James reached into his pocket. Drew and Ian watched him, silent. Collin watched his brothers.

"I want you to have one of these," the counselor said as he placed something in each of the younger boys' hands. It looked like a fish on a tiny chain. "It's a reminder of what I said, that God will watch over you."

Collin's curiosity made his palm itch to reach out, but he didn't. Instead, Mr. James had to pry his fingers apart and slide the fish-shaped piece of metal into the hollow of his hand.

Much as he wanted to, Collin refused to look at it. Better to cut to the chase and quit all this hype. "Where are we going this time?"

His stupid voice shook. He clenched his fists to still the trembling. The metal fish, warm from Mr. James's skin, bit into his flesh.

The pretty social worker looked up, startled that he'd spoken. Collin wondered if she could see the fury, red and hot, that pushed against the back of his eyes.

"We already have foster placements for Drew and Ian."

But not for him. The anger turned to fear. "Together?"

As long as they were together, they'd be okay.

"No. I'm sorry. Not this time."

He knew what she meant. He knew the system probably better than she did. Only certain people would take boys like Drew who expressed their anger. And nobody would take him. He was too old. People liked little and cute like Ian, not fighters, not runaways, not big boys with an attitude.

Panic shot through him, made his heart pound wildly. "They have to stay with me. Ian gets scared."

The social worker rose and touched his shoulder. "He'll be fine, Collin."

Collin shrugged away to glare at the brown paneled wall behind the counselor's desk. Helpless fury seethed inside him.

The worst had finally happened.

He and Drew and Ian were about to be separated.

# *Chapter One*

*Twenty-three years later, Oklahoma City*

Sweat burned his eyes, but Collin Grace didn't move. He couldn't. One wrong flinch and somebody died.

Totally focused on the life-and-death scenario playing out on the ground below, he hardly noticed the sun scalding the back of his neck or the sweat soaking through his protective vest.

The Tac-team leader's voice came through the earphone inside his Fritz helmet. "Hostage freed. Suspect in custody. Get down here for debrief."

Collin relaxed and lowered the .308 caliber marksman rifle, a SWAT sniper's best friend, and rose from his prone position on top of the River Street Savings and Loan. Below him, the rest of the team exited a training house and headed toward Sergeant Gerrara.

Frequent training was essential and Collin welcomed every drill. Theirs wasn't a full-time SWAT unit, so they had to stay sharp for those times when the callout would come and they'd have to act. Normally a patrol cop, he'd spent all morning on the firing range, requalifying with every weapon known to mankind. He was good. Real good, with the steadiest hands anyone on the force had ever seen. A fact that made him proud.

"You headed for the gym after this?" His buddy, fellow police officer and teammate, Maurice Johnson shared his propensity for exercise. Stay in shape, stay alive. Most special tactics cops agreed.

Collin peeled his helmet off and swiped a hand over his sweating brow. "Yeah. You?"

"For a few reps. I told Shanita I'd be home early. Bible study at our place tonight." Maurice sliced a sneaky grin in Collin's direction. Sweat dripped from his high ebony cheeks and rolled down a neck the size of a linebacker's. "Wanna come?"

Collin returned the grin with a shake of his head. Maurice wouldn't give up. He extended the same invitation every Thursday.

Collin liked Maurice and his family, but he couldn't see a loner like himself spouting Bible verses and singing in a choir. It puzzled him, too, that a cop as tough and smart as Maurice would feel the need for God. To Collin's way of thinking there was only one person he trusted enough to lean on. And that was himself.

"Phone call for you, Grace," Sergeant Gerrara hollered. "Probably some cutie after your money."

The other cops hooted as Collin shot Maurice an exasperated look and took off in a trot. He received plenty of teasing about his single status. Some of the guys tried to fix him up, but when a woman started pushing him or trying to get inside his head, she was history. He didn't need the grief.

The heavy tactics gear rattled and bounced against his body as he grabbed the cell phone from Sergeant Gerrara's over-size fist, trading it for his rifle.

"Grace."

"Sergeant Collin Grace?" A feminine voice, light and sweet, hummed against his ear.

"Yeah." He shoved his helmet under one arm and stepped away from the gaggle of cops who listened in unabashedly. "Who's this?"

"Mia Carano. I'm with the Cleveland County Department of Child Welfare."

A cord of tension stretched through Collin's chest. Adrenaline, just now receding from the training scenario, ratcheted up a notch. Child welfare, a department he both loathed and longed to hear from. Could it finally be news?

He struggled to keep his voice cool and detached. "Is this about my brothers?"

"Your brothers?"

Envisioning her puzzled frown, Collin realized she had no idea he'd spent years trying to find Ian and Drew. The spurt of energy drained out of him. "Never mind. What can I do for you, Ms. Carano?"

"Do you recall the young boy you picked up last week behind the pawn shop?"

"The runaway?" He could still picture the kid. "Angry, scared, but too proud to admit it?"

"Yes. Mitchell Perez. He's eleven. Going on thirty."

The kid hadn't looked a day over nine. Skinny. Black hair too long and hanging in his eyes. A pack of cigarettes crushed and crammed down in his jeans' pocket. He'd reminded Collin too much of Drew.

"You still got him? Or did he go home?"

"Home for now, but he's giving his mother fits."

From what the kid had told him, she deserved fits. "He'll run again."

"I know. That's why I'm calling you."

Around him the debrief was breaking up. He lifted a hand to the departing team.

"Nothing I can do until he runs."

He leaned an elbow against somebody's black pickup truck and watched cars pull up to a stop sign adjacent to the parking lot. Across the street, shoppers came and went in a strip mall. Normal, common occurrences in the city on a peaceful, sunny afternoon. Ever alert, he filed them away, only half listening to the caller.

"This isn't my first encounter with Mitch. He's a troubled boy, but his mother said you impressed him. He talks about you. Wants to be a cop."

Collin felt a con coming on. Social workers were good at that. He stayed quiet, let her ramble on in that sugary voice.

"He has no father. No male role model."

Big surprise. He switched the phone to the other ear.

"I thought you might be willing to spend some time with the boy. Perhaps through CAPS, our child advocate program. It's sort of like Big Brothers only through the court system."

He was already a big brother and he'd done a sorry job of that. Some of the other officers did that sort of outreach, but not him.

"I don't think so."

"At least give me a chance to talk with you about it. I have some other ideas if CAPS doesn't appeal."

He was sure she did. Her type always had ideas. "This isn't my kind of thing. Call the precinct. They might know somebody."

"Tell you what," she said as if he hadn't just turned her down. "Meet me at Chick's Place in fifteen minutes. I'll buy you a cup of coffee."

She didn't give up easy. She even knew the cops' favorite hamburger joint.

He didn't know why, but he said, "Make it forty-five minutes and a hamburger, onions fried."

She laughed and the sound was light, musical.

He liked it. It was her occupation that turned him off.

"I'll even throw in some cheese fries," she added.

"Be still my heart." He couldn't believe he'd said that. Regardless of her sweet voice, he didn't know this woman and didn't particularly want to.

"I'll sit in the first booth so you'll recognize me."

"What if it's occupied?"

"I'll buy them a burger, too." She laughed again. The sound ran over him like fresh summer rain. "See you in forty-five minutes."

The phone went dead and Collin stared down at it, puzzled that a woman—a social worker, no less—had conned him into meeting her for what was, no doubt, even more of a con.

Well, he had news for Mia Carano with the sweet voice. Collin Grace didn't con easy. Regardless of what she wanted, the answer was already no.

Mia recognized him the minute he walked in the door. No matter that the hamburger café was littered with uniformed police officers hunched over burgers or mega-size soft drinks. Collin Grace stood out in a crowd. Brown eyes full of caution swept the room once, as if calculating escape routes, before coming to rest on her. She prided herself on being able to read people. Sergeant Grace didn't trust a soul in the place.

"There he is," the middle-aged officer across from

her said, nodding toward the entrance. “That’s Amazin’ Grace.”

Mia fixed her attention on the lean, buff policeman coming her way. With spiked dark hair, slashing eyebrows and a permanent five o’clock shadow, he was good-looking in a hard, manly kind of way. His fatigue pants and fitted brown T-shirt with a Tac-team emblem over the heart looked fresh and clean as though he’d recently changed.

Officer Jess Snow pushed out of the booth he’d kindly allowed her to share. In exchange, he had regaled her with stories about the force, his grandkids, and his plan to retire next year. He’d also told her that the other policemen referred to the officer coming her way as Amazin’ Grace because of his uncanny cool and precision even under the most intense conditions. “Guess I’ll get moving. Sure was nice talking to you.”

She smiled up at the older man. “You, too, Jess.”

Officer Snow gave her a wink and nodded to the newcomer as he left.

Collin returned a short, curt nod and then jacked an eyebrow at Mia. “Miss Carano?”

A bewildering flutter tickled her stomach. “Yes, but I prefer Mia.”

As he slid into the booth across from her the equipment attached to his belt rattled and a faint stir of some warm, tangy aftershave pierced the scent of frying onions. She noted that he did not return the courtesy by asking her to use his given name.

She wasn't surprised. He was every bit the cool, detached cop. Years of looking at the negative side of life did that to some social workers as well. Mia was thankful she had the Lord and a very supportive family to pour out all her frustrations and sadness upon. Her work was her calling. She was right where God could best use her, and she'd long ago made up her mind not to let the dark side of life burn her out.

Sergeant Grace, on the other hand, might as well be draped in strips of yellow police tape that screamed, Caution: Restricted Area. Getting through his invisible shield wouldn't be as easy as she'd hoped.

He propped his forearms on the tabletop like a barrier between them. His left T-shirt sleeve slid upward to reveal the bottom curve of a tattoo emblazoned with a set of initials she couldn't quite make out.

Though she didn't move or change expressions, a part of her shrank back from him. She'd never understood a man's propensity to mutilate his arms with dye and needles.

"So," he said, voice deep and smooth. "What can I do for you, Mia?"

"Don't you want your hamburger first?"

The tight line of his mouth mocked her. "A spoonful of sugar doesn't really make the medicine go down any easier."

So cynical. And he couldn't be that much older

than she was. Early thirties maybe. "You might actually enjoy what I have in mind."

"I doubt it." He raised a hand to signal the waitress. "What would you like?" he asked.

She motioned to her Coke. "This is fine. I'm not hungry."

He studied her for a second before turning his attention to the waitress. "Bring me a Super Burger. Fry the onions, hold the tomatoes, and add a big order of cheese fries and a Mountain Dew."

The waitress poised with pen over pad and said in a droll voice, "What's the occasion? Shoot somebody today?"

One side of the policeman's mouth softened. He didn't smile, but he was close. "Only a smart-mouthed waitress. Nobody will miss her."

The waitress chuckled and said to Mia, "I never thought I'd see the day grease would cross his lips."

She sauntered away, hollering the order to a guy in the back.

"I thought all cops were junk-food junkies."

"It's the hours. Guys don't always have time to eat right."

"But you do?"

"Sometimes."

If he was a health food nut he wasn't going to talk to her about it. Curious the way he avoided small talk. Was he this way with everyone? Or just her?

Maybe it was her propensity for nosiness. Maybe

it was her talkative Italian heritage. But Mia couldn't resist pushing a little to see what he would do. "So what *do* you eat? Bean sprouts and yogurt?"

"Is that why you're here? To talk about my diet?"

So cold. So empty. Had she made a mistake in thinking this ice man might help a troubled boy?

On the other hand, Grandma Carano said still waters run deep. Gran had been talking about Uncle Vitorio, the only quiet Carano in the giant, noisy family, and she'd been right. Uncle Vitorio was a thinker, an inventor. Granted he mostly invented useless gadgets to amuse himself, but the family considered him brilliant and deep.

Perhaps Collin was the same. Or maybe he just needed some encouragement to loosen up.

She pushed her Coke to one side and got down to business.

"For some reason, Mitchell Perez has developed a heavy case of hero worship for you."

The boy was one of those difficult cases who didn't respond well to any of the case workers, the counselors or anybody else for that matter, but something inside Mia wouldn't give up. Last night, when she'd prayed for the boy, this idea to contact Collin Grace had come into her mind. She'd believed it was God-sent, but now she wondered.

"More and more in the social system we're seeing boys like Mitchell who don't have a clue how to become responsible, caring men. They need real men to teach them and to believe in them. Men they can relate to and admire."

The waitress slid a soda and a paper-covered straw in front of Sergeant Grace.

"How do you know I'm that kind of man?"

"I checked you out."

He tilted his head. "Just because I'm a good cop doesn't mean I'd be a suitable role model to some street kid."

"I'm normally a good judge of character and I think you would be. The thing here is need. We have so many needy kids, and few men willing to spend a few hours a week to make a difference. Don't you see, Officer? In the long run, your job will be easier if someone intercedes on behalf of these kids now. Maybe they won't end up in trouble later on down the road."

"And maybe they will."

Frustration made her want to pound the table. "You know the statistics. Mentored kids are less likely to get into drugs and crime. They're more likely to go to college. More likely to hold jobs and be responsible citizens. Don't you get it, Officer? A few hours a week of your time can change a boy's life."

He pointed his straw at her. "You haven't been at this long, have you?"

She blinked, leaned back in the booth and tried to calm down. "Seven years."

"Longer than I thought."

"Why? Because I care? Because I'm not burned out?"

"It happens." The shrug in his voice annoyed her.

"Is that what's happened to you?"

A pained look came and went on his face, but he kept silent—again.

Mia leaned forward, her passionate Italian nature taking control. "Look, this may not make any sense to you. Or it may sound idealistic, but I believe what I do makes a difference in these kids' lives."

"Maybe they don't want you to make a difference. Maybe they want to be left alone."

"Left alone? To be abused?"

"Not all of them are mistreated."

"Or neglected. Or cold and hungry, eating out of garbage cans."

Collin's face closed up tighter than a miser's fist. Had the man no compassion?

"There are a lot of troubled kids out there. Why are you so focused on this particular one?"

"I'm concerned about all of them."

"But?"

So he'd heard the hesitation.

"There's something special about Mitch." Something about the boy pulled at her, kept her going back to check on him. Kept her trying. "He wants to make it, but he doesn't know how."

Collin's expression shifted ever so slightly. The change was subtle, but Mia felt him softening. His eyes flicked sideways and, as if glad for the interruption, he said, “Food’s coming.”

The waitress slid the steaming burger and fries onto the table. “There you go. A year’s worth of fat and cholesterol.”

“No wonder Chick keeps you around, Millie. You’re such a great salesman.”

“Saleslady, thank you.”

He took a giant bite of the burger and sighed. “Perfect. Just like you.”

Millie rolled her eyes and moved on. Collin turned his attention back to Mia. “You were saying?”

“Were you even listening?”

“To every word. The kid is special. Why?”

Mia experienced a twinge of pleasure. Collin Grace confused her, but there was something about him…

“Beneath Mitch’s hard layer is a gentleness. A sweet little boy who doesn’t know who to trust or where to turn.”

“Imagine that. The world screws him over from birth and he stops trusting it. What a concept.”

The man was cool to the point of frostbite and had a shell harder than any of the street kids she dealt with. If she could crack this tough nut perhaps other cops would follow suit. She was already pursuing the idea of mentor groups through her church, but cops-as-mentors could make an impact like no other.

She took a big sip of Coke and then said, “At least talk to Mitch.”

The pager at Collin's waist went off. He slipped the device from his belt, glanced at the display, and pushed out of the booth, leaving a half-eaten burger and a nearly full basket of cheese fries.

Mia looked up at the tall and dark and distant cop. "Is that your job?"

He nodded curtly. "Gotta go. Thanks for the dinner."

"Could I call you about this later?"

"No point. The answer will still be no." He whipped around with the precision of a marine and strode out of the café before Mia could argue further.

Disappointment curled in her belly. When she could close her surprised mouth, she did so with a huff.

The basket of leftover fries beckoned. She crammed a handful in her mouth. No use wasting perfectly good cheese fries. Even if they did end up on her hips.

Sergeant Collin Grace may have said no, but no didn't always mean absolutely no.

And Mia wasn't quite ready to give up on Mitchell Perez…or Collin Grace.

## *Chapter Two*

"Hey Grace, you spending the night here or something?"

Eyes glued to the computer screen, Collin lifted a finger to silence the other cop. "Gotta check one more thing."

His shift was long over, and the sun drifted toward the west, but at least once a week he checked and rechecked, just in case he'd missed something the other five thousand times he'd searched.

Somewhere out there he had two brothers, and with the explosion of information on the Internet he would find them—eventually. After all this time, though, he wasn't expecting a miracle.

His cell phone played the University of Oklahoma fight song and he glanced down at the caller ID. Her again. Mia Carano. She'd left no less than ten messages over the past three days. He had talked to her twice, told her no and then hadn't bothered to return her other calls. Eventually she'd get the message.

The rollicking strains of "Boomer Sooner" faded away as his voice mail picked up. Collin kept his attention on the computer screen.

Over the years, he'd amassed quite a list of names and addresses. One by one, he'd checked them out and moved them to an inactive file. He typed several more names into the file on his computer and hit Save.

The welfare office suggested he should hire a private search agency, but Collin never planned to do that. The idea of letting someone else poke into his troubled background made him nervous. He'd done a good job of leaving that life behind and didn't want the bones of his childhood dug up by some stranger.

Part of the frustration in this search, though, lay with his own limited memory. Given what he knew of his mother, he wasn't even sure he and his brothers shared a last name. And even if they once had, either or both could have been changed through adoption.

Maurice Johnson, staying late to finish a report, bent over Collin's desk. "Any luck?"

He kept his voice low, and Collin appreciated his discretion. It was one of the reasons he'd confided in his coworker and friend about the missing brothers. It was also one of the reasons the man was one of his few close friends. Maurice knew how to keep his mouth shut.

"Same old thing. I added a few more men with the

last names of Grace and Stotz, my mother's maiden name, to the list, but I'm convinced the boys were moved out of Oklahoma after we were separated."

Their home state had been a dead end from the get-go.

"Any luck in the Texas system?"

"Not yet. But it's huge. Finding the names is easy. Matching ages and plundering records isn't quite as simple."

"Even for a cop."

A lot of the old files were not even computerized yet. And even if he could find them, there were plenty of records he couldn't access.

"Yeah. If only most adoption records weren't sealed. Or there was a centralized listing of some sort."

"Twenty years ago record-keeping wasn't the art it is today."

"Tell me about it."

He'd stuck his name and information on a number of legit sibling searches. He'd even placed a letter in his old welfare file in case one of the boys was also searching.

Apparently, his brothers weren't all that eager to make contact. Either that or something had happened to them. His gut clenched. Better not travel that line of thinking.

"Did you ever consider that you might have other family out there? A grandma, an aunt. Somebody."

He shook his head. "Hard as I've tried, I don't

remember anyone. If we ever had any family, Mama had long since alienated them."

He'd had stepdads and "uncles" aplenty. He even remembered Ian's dad as a pretty good guy, but the only name he'd ever called the man was Rob.

A few years back he'd tracked his mother down in Seminole County—in jail for public intoxication. His lips twisted at the memory. She'd been too toasted to give false information and for once one of her real names, anyway a name Collin remembered, appeared on the police bulletin.

Their subsequent visit had not been a joyous reunion of mother and son. And, to his great disappointment, she knew less about his brothers' whereabouts than he did.

After that, she had disappeared off the radar screen again. Probably moved in with her latest party man and changed her name for the tenth or hundredth time. Not that Collin cared. It was his brothers he wanted to find. Karen Stotz-Grace-Whatever had given them birth, but if she'd ever been a mother he didn't remember it.

"Do you think they're together?"

"Ian and Drew? No." He remembered that last day too clearly. "They were headed to different foster homes. Chances are they weren't reunited either."

His mother hadn't bothered to jump through the welfare hoops anymore after that. She'd let the state have custody of all three of them. Collin, who ended up in a group home, had failed in his promise to take care of his brothers. He hoped they had been adopted. He hoped they'd found decent, loving families to give them what he hadn't been able to. Even though they were grown men, he needed to know if they were all right.

And if they weren't...

He got that heavy, sick feeling in the pit of his stomach and logged out of the search engine.

Leaning back in the office chair, he scraped a hand over his face and said, "Think I'll call it a night."

Maurice clapped him on the shoulder. "Come by the house. Shanita will make you a fruit smoothie, and Thomas will harangue you for a game of catch."

"Thanks. But I can't. Gotta get out to the farm." He rose to his feet, stretching to relieve the ache across his mid-back. "The vet's coming by to check that new pup."

"How's he doing?" The other cops were suckers for animals just as he was. They just didn't take their concern quite as far.

"Still in the danger zone." Fury sizzled his blood every time he thought of the abused pup. "Even after what happened, he likes people."

"Animals are very forgiving," Maurice said.

Collin pushed the glass door open with one hand, holding it for his friend to pass through. Together they left the station and walked through the soft evening breeze to the parking garage.

"Unlike me. If I find out who tied that little fella's

legs with wire and left him to die, I'll be tempted to return the favor."

Another police officer had found the collie mix, but not before one foot was amputated and another badly infected. And yet, the animal craved human attention and affection.

They entered the parking garage, footsteps echoing on the concrete, the shady interior cool and welcome. Exhaust fumes hovered in the dimness like smelly ghosts.

Maurice dug in his pocket, keys rattling. "Did your social worker call again today?"

Collin slowed, eyes narrowing. "How did you know?"

His buddy lifted a shoulder. "She has friends in high places."

Great. "The department can't force me to do something like that."

"You take in wounded animals. Why not wounded kids?"

"Not my thing."

"Because it hits too close to home?"

Collin stopped next to his Bronco, pushed the lock release, and listened for the snick.

"I don't need reminders." Enough memories plagued him without that. "You like kids. You do it."

"Someday you're going to have to forgive the past, Collin. Lay it to rest. I know Someone who can help you with that."

Collin recognized the subtle reference to God and let it slide. Though he admired the steadfast faith he saw in Maurice, he wasn't sure what he believed when it came to religion. He fingered the small metal fish in his pocket, rubbing the ever-present scripture that was his one and only connection to God. And to his brothers.

"Nothing to forgive. I just don't like thinking about it."

Maurice looked doubtful but he didn't argue. The quiet acceptance was another part of the man's character Collin appreciated. He said his piece and then shut up.

"This social worker. Her name's Carano, right?"

Collin glanced up, surprised. His grip tightened on the metal door handle. "Yeah."

"She goes to my church."

Collin suppressed a groan. "Don't turn on me, man."

He'd had enough trouble getting Mia Carano out of his head without Maurice weighing in on the deal. The social worker was about the prettiest thing he'd seen in a long time. She emanated a sincere decency that left him unsettled about turning her down, but hearing her smooth, sweet voice on his voice mail a dozen times a day was starting to irritate him.

"Single. Nice family." White teeth flashed in Maurice's dark face. "Easy on the eyes."

Was she ever! Like an ad for an Italian restaurant. Heavy red-brown hair that swirled around her shoulders. Huge, almond-shaped gray-green eyes. A wide, happy mouth. Not too skinny either. He never had gone for ultra-thin women. Made him think they were hungry.

"I didn't notice."

"You're cool, Grace, but you ain't dead."

"Don't start, Johnson. I'm not interested. A woman like that would talk a man to pieces." Wasn't she already doing as much?

Maurice chuckled and moseyed off toward his car. His deep voice echoed through the concrete dungeon. "Sooner or later, boy, one of them's gonna get you."

Collin waved him off, climbed into his SUV, and cranked the gas-guzzling engine to life. Nobody was going to "get" him. Way he figured, nobody wanted a hard case like him. And that was fine. The only people he really wanted in his life were his brothers. Wherever they were.

Pulling out of the dark underground, he headed west toward the waning sun. The acreage five miles out of the city was a refuge, both for the animals and for him.

His cell phone rang again. Sure enough, it was the social worker. He shook his head and kept driving.

The veterinarian's dually turned down the short dirt driveway directly behind Collin. The six-wheeled pickup, essential for the rugged places a vet had to traverse, churned up dust and gravel.

"Good timing," Collin muttered to the rearview

mirror, glad not to be in back of Doc White's mini dust storm, but also glad to see the dependable animal doctor.

If Paige White said she'd be here, she was. With her busy practice, sometimes she didn't arrive until well after dark, but she always arrived. Collin figured the woman worked more hours than anyone he knew.

The vet followed Collin past the half-built house he called home to the bare patches of grass that served as parking spots in front of a weathered old barn.

A string of fenced pens, divided according to species, dotted the space behind the barn. In one, a pair of neglected and starved horses was slowly regaining strength. In another, a deer healed from an arrow wound.

To one side, a rabbit hutch held a raccoon. And inside the small barn were five dogs, three cats and ten kittens. He was near capacity. As usual. He needed to add on again, but he also needed to continue the work on his house. The bank wouldn't loan money on two rooms, a bathroom and a concrete slab framed in wood.

Booted feet first, the vet leaped from the high cab of her truck with a whoop for a greeting.

"Hey there, ornery. How's business?" she hollered as Collin came around the front of his SUV.

"Which one?"

"The only one that counts." She waved a gloved hand toward the barn, and Collin nearly smiled. Paige

White, a forty-something cowgirl with a heart as big and warm as the sun, joked that animals liked her faster, better and longer than humans ever had.

One thing Collin knew for sure, animals responded to her treatment. He fell in step with the short, sturdy blond and headed inside the barn.

Without preliminary, he said, "The pup's leg smells funny."

"You been cleaning those wounds the way I showed you?"

"Every day." He remembered the first time he'd poured antiseptic cleaner on the pup's foot and listened to its pitiful cries.

Doc stopped, stared at him for a minute and then said, "We'll have a look at him first."

Paige White could always read his concern, though he had a poker face. Her uncanny sixth sense would have bothered him under other circumstances.

The scent of fresh straw and warm-blooded animals astir beneath their feet, they reached the stall where the collie was confined.

From a large, custom-cut cardboard box, the pup gazed at them with dark, moist, delighted eyes. His shaggy tail thumped madly at the side of the box.

As always, Collin marveled at the pup's adoring welcome. He'd been cruelly treated by humans and yet his love didn't falter.

Doc knelt down, crooning. "How's my pal today? Huh? How ya doin', boy?"

"I call him Happy."

"Well, Happy." The dog licked her extended hand, the tail thumping faster. "Let me see those legs of yours." She jerked her chin at Collin, who'd hunkered down beside her. "Make sure this guy over here's looking after you."

With exquisite tenderness, she inspected one limb and then the other. Her pale eyebrows slammed together as she examined the deep, ugly wound.

Collin watched, anxious, when she took a hypodermic from her long, leather bag and filled it with medication.

"What's that?"

"More antibiotic." She held the syringe at eye level and flicked the plastic several times. "I don't like the way this looks, Collin. There's not enough tissue left to debride."

"Meaning?"

"We may have to take this foot off, too."

"Ah, man." He scrubbed a hand over his face, heard his whiskers. He knew Paige would fight hard to avoid another amputation, so if she brought up the subject, she wasn't blowing smoke. "Any hope?"

"Where there's life, there's hope. But if he doesn't respond to treatment soon, we'll have to remove the foot to save him. Infection like this can spread to the entire body in a hurry."

"I know. But a dog with two amputated feet…"

He let the thought go. Doc knew the odds of the

pup having any quality of life. Finding a home for him would be close to impossible, and Collin only kept the animals until they were healthy and adoptable or ready to return to the wild. He didn't keep pets. Just animals in need.

Doc dropped the empty syringe into a plastic container, then patted his shoulder. "Don't fret. I'll run out again tomorrow. Got Jenner's Feed Store to donate their broken bags of feed to you and I want to be here to see them delivered. Clovis Jenner owes me."

Warmth spread through Collin's chest. "So do I."

Doc was constantly on the look-out for feed, money, any kind of support she could round up for his farm. And she only charged him for supplies or medications, never for her expertise.

"Nonsense. If it wasn't for me and my soft heart, you wouldn't have all these critters. I just can't put them down without trying."

"I know." He felt the same way. Whenever she called with a stray animal in need of a place to heal, Collin took it if he had room. He was stretched to the limit on space and funds, but he had to keep going. "Let's go check on the others."

Together they made the rounds. She checked the cats and dogs first, redressing wounds, giving shots, poking pills down resistant throats, instructing Collin on the next phase of care.

At the horses' pen, she nodded her approval and pushed a tube of medication down each scrawny throat. "They're more alert. See how this one lifts her head now to watch us? That's a very good sign."

One of the mares, Daisy, leaned her velvety nose against Collin's shirtfront and snuffled. In return for her affection, he stroked her neck, relishing the warm, soft feel against his fingers.

The first few days after the horses had arrived, Collin had come out to the barn every four hours to follow the strict refeeding program Doc had put them on. Seeing the horses slowly come back from the brink of death made the sleepless nights and interrupted days worth the effort.

Sometimes the local Future Farmers of America kids helped out. The other cops occasionally did the same. Most of the time, Collin preferred to work alone.

At the raccoon's hutch, Paige declared the hissing creature fit and ready to release. And finally, she stood at the fence and watched the young buck limp listlessly around the pen.

"He's depressed."

"Deer get depressed?"

"Mmm. Trauma, pain, fear lead to depression in any species." She squinted into the gathering darkness, intelligent eyes studying every move the deer made. "The wound looks good though."

"You do good work."

Some bow hunter had shot the buck. He had escaped with an arrow protruding from his hip, finally collapsing near enough to a house that dogs had alerted the owner. Paige had operated on the badly infected hip.

"I do, don't I?" The vet smiled smugly before sobering. "Only time will tell if enough muscle remains for him to survive in the wild, though."

She turned and started back around the barn to her truck. Collin took her bag and followed.

Headlights sliced the dusk and came steadily toward them, the hum of a motor loud against the quiet country evening.

Collin tensed. "Company," he said.

"Who is it?"

"My favorite neighbor," he said, sarcasm thicker than the cloud of dust billowing around the car. "Cecil Slokum."

Collin and his farm were located a half mile from the nearest house, but Slokum harassed him on a regular basis with some complaint about the animals.

The late-model brown sedan pulled to a stop. A man the size and shape of Danny DeVito put the engine in Park and rolled down a window. His face was red with anger.

"I'm not putting up with this anymore, Grace."

The sixth sense that made Collin a good cop kicked in. He made a quick survey of the car's interior, saw no weapons and relaxed a little.

"What's the problem, Mr. Slokum?" He sounded way more polite than he felt.

“One of them dogs of yours took down my daughter’s prize ewe last night.”

“Didn’t happen.” All his animals were sick and in pens.

“Just ’cause you’re a big shot cop don’t make you right. I know what I saw.”

“Wasn’t one of mine.”

“Tell it to the judge.” The man shoved a brown envelope out the window.

Collin took it, puzzled. “What is this?”

“See for yourself.” With that, Slokum crammed the car into gear and backed out, disappearing down the gravel road much more quickly than he’d come.

Collin stared down at the envelope.

“Might as well open it,” Doc said.

With a shrug, Collin tore the seal, pulled out a legal-looking sheet of vellum and read. When he finished, he slammed a fist against the offending form.

Just what he needed right now. Someone else besides the annoying social worker on his back.

“Collin?” Doc said.

Jaw rigid, he handed her the paper and said, “Nothing like good neighbors. The jerk is suing me for damages.”

# *Chapter Three*

Mia perched on a high kitchen stool, swiveling back and forth, her mind a million miles away from her mother's noisy kitchen as she sliced boiled zucchini for stuffing.

At the stove, Grandma Maria Celestina stirred her special marinara sauce while Mama prepared the sausages for baked ziti.

The rich scents of tomato and basil and sausages had the whole family prowling in and out of the kitchen.

"Church was good today, huh, Mia?"

"Good, Mama."

At fifty-six, Rosalie Carano was still a pretty woman. People said Mia favored her and she hoped so. She'd always thought Mama looked like Sophia Loren. Flowered apron around her generous hips, Rosalie sailed around the large family kitchen with the efficient energy that had successfully raised five kids.

The whole clan gathered every Sunday after church for a late-afternoon meal of Mama's traditional Italian cooking, which always included breads and pastries from the family bakery. In the living room, her dad, Leo, argued basketball with her eldest brother Gabe and Grandpa Salvatore. Gabe's wife, Abby, had taken their two kids outside to swim in the above-ground pool accompanied by Mia's pregnant sister, Anna Maria. The other brothers, Adam and Nic, roamed in and out of the kitchen like starving ten-year-olds.

Mia was blessed with a good family. Not perfect by any means, but close and caring. She appreciated that, especially on days like today when she felt inexplicably down in the dumps. Even church service, which usually buoyed her spirits, had left her uncharacteristically quiet.

Collin Grace had not returned one of her phone calls in the past three days, and she'd practically promised Mitchell that he would. She disliked pulling in favors, tried not to use her eldest brother's influence as a city councilman, but Sergeant Grace was a tough nut to crack.

Nic, her baby brother, snitched a handful of grated mozzarella from the bowl at her elbow. Out of habit, she whacked his hand then listened to the expected howl of protest.

"Go away," she muttered.

His grin was unrepentant. At twenty, dark and

athletic Nic was a chick magnet. He knew his charms, though they had never worked on either of his sisters.

"You're grumpy."

Brother Adam hooked an elbow around her neck and yanked back. She tilted her head to look up at him. Adam Carano, dark and tall, was eleven months older than Mia. From childhood, they'd been best friends, and he could read her like the Sunday comics.

"What's eating you, sis? You're too quiet. It scares me." He usually complained that she talked too much.

Gabe stuck his head around the edge of the door. "Last time she was quiet, Nic and Adam ended up with strange new haircuts."

Mia rolled her eyes. "I was eight."

"And we've not had a moment of peace and quiet from you since," Adam joked.

"And I," Nic put in, "was scarred for life at the ripe old age of one."

"I should have cut off your tongue."

"Mom," Nic called in a whiney little-boy voice. "Mia's picking on me."

Mia ignored him and set to work stuffing the zucchini boats.

"What is it, Mia?" Mama asked. "Adam's right. You are not yourself."

"It's a kid," Adam replied before she could. "It's always one of her kids."

Mia pulled a face. He knew her so well. "Smarty."

Mama shushed him. "Let her tell us. Maybe we can help."

It was Mama's way. If one of her chicks had a problem, the mother hen rushed in to fix it—bringing with her lasagna or cookies. So Mia told them about Mitch.

"He's salvageable, Mama. There is a lot of good in him, but he needs a man's influence and guidance. I tried getting him into the Big Brothers program but he refuses."

"One of the boys will talk to him. Won't you, boys?" Rosalie eyed her three sons with a look that brooked no argument.

"Sure. Of course we would." All three men nodded in unison like bobble toys in the back window of a car.

Heart filling with love for these overgrown macho teddy bears she called brothers, Mia shook her head. "Thanks, guys. You're the best. But Mitch is distrustful of most people. He'd never agree. For some reason, he zeroed in on one of the street patrolmen and will only talk to him. The cop is perfect, but—"

"Whoo-oo, Mia found her a perfect man. Go, sis." The brothers started in with the catcalls and bad jokes.

When the noise subsided, she said, "Not that kind of perfect, unfortunately. I don't even like the guy."

But she couldn't get him out of her mind either.

"Mia!"

"Oh, Mama." Mia plopped the last zucchini boat on a pan and sprinkled parmesan on top. "Our first meeting was disastrous. I bought the man a hamburger to soften him up a little, and he didn't even stick around long enough to eat it. And now he doesn't bother to return my phone calls."

"You've lost your charm, sis. Need some lessons?" Nic flexed both arms and preened around the kitchen, bumping into Grandma who, in turn, shook a gnarled finger in his laughing face.

Rosalie whirled and flapped her apron at the men. "Out. Shoo. We'll never get dinner on."

Gabe and Nic disappeared, still laughing. Adam stayed behind, pulled a stool around the bar with one foot, and perched beside Mia.

The most Italian-looking of the Carano brothers, Adam was swarthy and handsome and a tad more serious than his siblings.

"Want me to beat him up?"

"Who? Mitch or the cop?"

He lifted a wide shoulder. "Either. Say the word."

"Maybe later."

They both grinned at the familiar joke. All through high school Adam had threatened to beat up any guy who made her unhappy. Though he'd never done it, the boys in her class had thought he would.

"If I could only convince Sergeant Grace to spend one day with Mitch, I think he'd be hooked.

He comes off as cold and uncaring, but I don't think he is."

"Some people aren't kid-crazy like you are. Especially us men types."

"All I want is a few hours a week of his time to save a kid from an almost certain future of crime and drugs." Mama swished by and took the pan of zucchini boats. "The couple of times I managed to get him on the phone, he barely said three words."

Adam swiveled her stool so that her back was to him. Strong hands massaged her shoulders.

"The guy was short and to the point. *No.* The least he could do is explain *why* he refuses, but he clams up like Uncle Vitorio."

Adam chuckled. "And that drives you nuts in a hurry."

"Yes, it does. Human beings have the gift of language. They should use it." She let her head go lax. "That feels good."

"You're tight as a drum."

"I didn't sleep much last night. I couldn't get Mitch off my mind so I got up to pray. And then, the next thing I know I'm praying for Collin Grace, too."

"The cop?"

"Yes. There's something about him…sort of an aloneness, I guess, that bothers me. I can't figure him out."

Adam squeezed her shoulders hard. "There's your trouble, sis. You always want to talk and analyze and dig until you know everything. Some people like to keep their books closed."

"You think so?" She swiveled back around to face him. "You think I'm too nosey? That I talk too much?"

"Yep. Pushy, too."

"Gabe thinks I'm too soft."

"That's because he's the pushiest lawyer in three states."

Didn't she know it? She'd lost her first job because of Gabe, and though he'd done everything in his power to make it up to her in the years since, Mia would never forget the humiliation of having her professional ethics compromised.

Nic stuck his head into the kitchen, then ducked when his mother threw a tea towel at him. "Mia, your purse is ringing. Should I get it?"

Mia slid off the stool and started toward the living room. She might be pushy, but she played fair.

A large masculine hand attached to a hairy arm—Nic's—appeared around the door, holding out the cell phone.

Taking it, Mia pushed the button and said, "Hello."

"Miss Carano, this is Monica Perez."

"Mrs. Perez, is something wrong?" Mia tensed. Today was Sunday. A strange time for calls from a client. "Is it Mitchell?"

The woman's voice sounded more weary than worried. "He's run away again. This time the worthless little creep stole money out of my purse."

* * *

Collin kicked back the roller chair and plopped down at his desk. He'd just returned from transporting a prisoner and had to complete the proper paperwork. Paperwork. Blah. Most Sundays he spent at the farm or crashed out on his couch watching ballgames. But this was his weekend to work.

"I need to see Sergeant Grace, please."

Collin recognized the cool, sweet voice immediately. Mia Carano, social worker to the world and nag of the first order, was in the outer office.

"Dandy," he muttered. "Make my day."

Tossing down the pen, he rose and strode toward the door just as she sailed through it. She looked fresh and young in tropical-print capris and an orange T-shirt, a far cry from the business suit and heels of their first meeting.

"Mitch has run away again," she blurted without preliminary.

"Nothing the police can do for twenty-four hours."

"We have to find him. I'm afraid he'll get into trouble again."

"Probably will."

Her gray-green eyes snapped with fire. "I want you to go with me to find him right now. I have some ideas where he might go, but he won't listen to me. He'll listen to you."

The woman was unbelievable. Like a bulldog, she never gave up.

"It's not police business."

"Can't you do something just because it's right? Because a kid out there needs you?"

Collin felt himself softening. Had any social worker ever worked this hard for him or his brothers?

"If I take a drive around, have a look in a couple places, will you leave me alone?"

"Probably not." Her pretty smile stretched wide beneath a pair of twinkling eyes.

She was a pest. An annoying, pretty, sweet, aggravating pest who would probably go right on driving him nuts until he gave in.

Against his better judgment, he reached into a file cabinet and yanked out a form. "Sign this."

"What is it?"

"Department policy. If you're riding in my car, you gotta sign."

The pretty smile grew wider—and warmer.

He was an idiot to do this. Her kind never stopped at one favor.

Without bothering to read the forms that released the police department of liability in case of injury, Mia scribbled her name on the line and then beat him out of the station house. At the curb, she stopped to look at him. He motioned toward his patrol car and she jumped into the passenger's seat. A gentle floral scent wafted on the breeze when she slammed the door. He never noticed things like that and it bugged him.

He also noticed that the inside of his black-and-white was a mess. A clipboard, ticket pad, a travel mug and various other junk littered the floorboards. Usually a neat freak, he wanted to apologize for the mess, but he kept stubbornly silent. Let her think what she liked. Let her think he was a slob. Why should he care what Mia Carano thought of him?

If she was bothered, she didn't say so. But she did talk. And talk. She filled him in on Mitch's likes and dislikes, his grades in school, the places he hung out. And then she started in on the child advocate thing. She told him how desperately the kid needed a strong male in his life. That he was a good kid, smart, funny and kind. A computer whiz at school.

This time there was no Delete button to silence her. Trapped inside the car, Collin had to listen.

He put on his signal, made a smooth turn onto Tenth Street and headed east toward the boy's neighborhood. "How do you know so much about this one kid?"

"His mom, his classmates, his teachers."

"Why?"

"It's my job."

"To come out on Sunday afternoon looking for a runaway?"

"His mother called me."

"Bleeding heart," he muttered.

"Better than being heartless."

He glanced sideways. "You think I'm heartless?"

She glared back. "Aren't you?"

No, he wasn't. But let her think what she would. He wasn't getting involved with anything to do with the social welfare system.

His radio crackled to life. A juvenile shoplifter.

Mia sucked in a distressed breath, the first moment of quiet they'd had.

Collin radioed his location and took the call.

"It's Mitchell," Mia said after hearing the details. "The description and area fit perfectly."

Heading toward the complainant's convenience store, Collin asked, "You got a picture of him?"

"Of course." She rummaged in a glittery silver handbag and stuck a photo under his nose.

Collin spotted the 7-Eleven up ahead. This woman surely did vex him.

He pulled into the concrete drive and parked in the fire lane.

"Stay here. I'll talk to the owner, get what information I can, and then we'll go from there."

The obstinate social worker pushed open her door and followed him inside the convenience store. She whipped out her picture of the Perez kid and showed it to the store owner.

"That's him. Comes in here all the time. I been suspicious of him. Got him on tape this time."

Collin filled out the mandatory paperwork, jotting down all the pertinent information. "What did he take?"

The owner got a funny look on his face. "He took weird stuff. Made me wonder."

Mia paced back and forth in front of the counter. "What kind of weird stuff?"

Collin silenced her with a stare. She widened rebellious eyes at him, but hushed—for the moment.

"Peroxide, cotton balls, a roll of bandage."

Mia's eyes widened even further. "Was he hurt?"

The owner shrugged. "What do I care? He stole from me."

"He's hurt. I just know it. We have to find him."

Collin shot her another look before saying to the clerk, "Anything else we should know?"

"Well, he did pay for the cat food." The man shifted uncomfortably and Collin suspected there was more to the story, but he wouldn't get it from this guy. He motioned to Mia and they left.

Once in the car, he said, "Any ideas?"

She crossed her arms. "You mean, I have permission to talk now?"

Collin stifled a grin. The annoying woman was also cute. "Be my guest."

"I know several places around here where kids hang out."

He knew a few himself. "I doubt he'll be in plain sight, but we can try."

He put the car in gear and drove east. They tried all the usual spots, the parks, the parking lots. They showed the kid's picture in video stores and to other kids on the streets, but soon ran out of places to look.

"We have to find him before he gets into more trouble."

"I doubt he'd come this far. We're nearly to the city dump."

As soon as he said the words, Collin knew. A garbage dump was exactly the kind of place he would have hidden when he was eleven.

With a spurt of adrenaline, he kicked the patrol car up and sped along the mostly deserted stretch of highway on the outskirts of the city.

When he turned onto the road leading to the landfill, Mia said incredulously, "You think he's here? In the city dump?"

He shot her an exasperated look. "Got a better idea?"

"No."

Collin slammed out of the car and climbed to the top of the enormous cavity. The stench rolled over him in waves.

"Ew." Beside him, Mia clapped a hand over her nose.

"Wait in the car. I'll look around."

Collin wasn't the least surprised when she ignored him.

"You go that way." She pointed left. "I'll take the right side."

Determination in her stride, she took off through the trash heap apparently unconcerned about her white shoes or clean clothes. Collin watched her go. A pinch of admiration tugged at him. He'd say one thing for Miss Social Worker, she wasn't a quitter.

His boots slid on loose dirt as he carefully picked his way down the incline. Some of the trash had been recently buried, but much more lay scattered about.

He watched his step, aware that among the discarded furniture and trash bags, danger and disease lurked. This was not a place for a boy. Unless that boy had no place else to turn.

His chest constricted. He'd been here and done this. Maybe not in this dump, but he understood what the kid was going through. He hated the memories. Hated the heavy pull of dread and hurt they brought.

This was why he didn't want to get involved with Mia's project. And now here he was, knee-deep in trash and recollections, moving toward what appeared to be a shelter of some sort.

Plastic trash bags that stretched across a pair of ragged-out couches were anchored in place by rocks, car parts, a busted TV set. An old refrigerator clogged one end and a cardboard box the other.

Mia was right. The kid had smarts. He'd built his hideout in an area unlikely to be buried for a while and had made the spot blend in with the rest of the junk.

As quietly as he could, Collin leaned down and

slid the cardboard box away. What he saw inside made his chest ache.

The kid had tried to make a home inside the shelter. An old blanket and a sack of clothes were piled on one end of a ragged couch. A flashlight lay on an up-turned crate. Beneath the crate, the kid had stored the canned milk, a jar of water, cat food and a box of cereal.

In the dim confines Mitchell knelt over a cardboard box, cotton ball and peroxide in hand.

Collin had a pretty good idea what was inside the box.

At the sudden inflow of light, the kid's head whipped around. A mix of fear and resentment widened his dark eyes.

"Nice place you got here," Collin said, stooping to enter.

"I'm not doing anything wrong."

"Stealing from convenience stores isn't wrong?"

"I had to. Panda—" Mitchell glanced down at the box "—she's hurt."

Curiosity aroused, Collin moved to the boy's side. A mother cat with three tiny kittens mewed up at him. Mitchell stroked the top of her head and she began to purr.

Collin's heart slammed against his ribs.

Oh, man. Déjà vu all over again.

"Mind if I take a look?"

The kid scooted sideways but hovered protectively.

Collin frowned. The cat was speckled with round burns, several of them clearly infected. "What happened?"

"Some kids had her. Mean kids who like to hurt things. She was their cat, but I took her when they started—"

Collin held up a hand. He didn't need the ugly details to visualize what the kid had saved the cat from.

"You can't stay here, Mitchell. Your mother is worried."

"She's just worried about her ten bucks."

"You shouldn't have taken it."

The kid shrugged, didn't answer, but Collin's own eyes told him where the money had gone. And if his nose was an indicator, the kid had scavenged a pack of cigarettes somewhere too which would explain the store owner's guilty behavior. He'd probably sold cigarettes to a minor.

"I'm not going back to her house."

"You have to."

"I can't. Panda and her babies will die if I don't take care of her. Archie, too."

"Archie?"

The kid reached behind them to the other couch and gently lifted a turtle out of a shoe box. A piece of silver duct tape ran along a fracture in the green shell.

Emotions swamped Collin. He felt as if he was being sucked under a whirlpool. Memories flashed through his head so fast he thought he was going blind.

At that moment, little Miss Social Worker poked her head through the opening. "I thought I heard voices."

Mitchell shrank away from her, blocking the box of cats with his body.

"I won't leave her," he said belligerently. "You can't make me."

"Maybe your mother will let you keep them," Collin said, hoping Mitchell's mother was better than he suspected.

"I'm not going back there, I said. Never."

"Why not?"

The boy's face closed up tight, a look Collin recognized all too well. Something ugly needed to be said and the kid wasn't ready to deal with it.

As the inevitability of the situation descended upon him, Collin pulled a hand down his face.

After a minute of pulling himself together, he spoke. "Nothing's going to happen to your cat. You have my word."

Mitch's face lightened, though distrust continued to ooze out of him. "How can you be sure?"

"Because," Collin said, wishing there was a way he could avoid involvement and knowing he couldn't, "I'll take her home with me."

The boy's face crumpled, incredulous. The belligerent attitude fled, replaced by the awful yearning of hope. "You will?"

"I know a good vet. Panda will be okay."

Mia ducked under the black plastic and came

inside. Her eyes glowed with pleasure. "That's really nice of you, Sergeant Grace."

"Yeah. That's me. Real nice." Stupid, too.

He was a cop. Tough. Hardened to the ugliness of humanity. He could resist about anything. Anything, that is, except looking at Mitch's face and seeing his own reflection.

Like it or not, he was about to become a big brother—again.

He only hoped he didn't mess it up this time around.

# *Chapter Four*

Mitchell sat huddled in the back seat of the patrol car, tense and suspicious. The cardboard carton containing cat, kittens and turtle rested on the seat beside him. The rest of his property was in a battered paint bucket on the floor.

"I told you I'm not going back there."

Mia turned in her seat, antennae going up. "Why not? Is something wrong at home?"

The boy ignored her.

Ever the cop, Collin spoke up. "Juvie Hall is the other alternative."

"Better than home."

The adults exchanged glances.

Collin hadn't said two complete sentences since they'd left Mitch's lean-to. He'd simply gathered up the animals and the rag-tag assortment of supplies and led the way to the cruiser. Mitchell had followed along without a fuss, his only concern for the animals. For some reason that Mia could not fathom, the two silent males seemed to communicate without words.

Right now, though, Collin's words were not helping. Mia stifled the urge to shush him. Something was amiss with the child and he was either too scared or too proud to say so.

She pressed a little harder. "I wish you'd talk to me, Mitch. I can help. It's what I do. If there is a problem at home I can help get it resolved."

Dirt spewed up over the windshield as they bumped and jostled down the dusty road out of the landfill. Once on the highway, Collin flipped on the windshield washers.

"How do you and your mother get along? Any problems there?"

Mitch turned his profile toward her and stared at the spattering water.

Mia softened her voice. "Mitch, if there's abuse, you need to tell me."

His head whipped around, expression fierce. "Leave my mom out of this."

Whoa! "Okay. What about your stepdad?"

Collin gave her a sideways glance that said he wished she'd shut up. She didn't plan on doing that any time soon. Something was wrong in this boy's life. Otherwise, he wouldn't be running away. He wouldn't be shoplifting, and he wouldn't dread going home. She would be a lousy social worker and an even worse human being if she didn't investigate the very real possibility of abuse.

"Mitchell," she urged softly. "You can trust me. I want to help."

The cruiser slowed to a turn, pulled through a concrete drive and stopped. Mitchell jerked upright. His eyes widened in fright.

"Hey. What are we doing here?"

The green-and-red sign of the 7-Eleven convenience store loomed above the gas pumps. Mia recognized it as the store from which Mitch had shoplifted. Facing consequences was an important part of teaching a child right from wrong, but Mia still felt sorry for him. And she felt frustrated to be getting nowhere in their conversation.

Collin shifted into Park and got out of the car.

Mitchell shrank back against the seat. "I ain't going in there."

Mia braced for a strong-armed confrontation between the cop and the kid, prepared to intervene if necessary. But the cop surprised her.

He opened the back door, hunkered down beside the car and spoke quietly, almost gently, to the scared boy. "Everybody messes up sometime, Mitch. Part of being a man means facing up to your mistakes. Are you willing to be a man about it?"

Although Mia was dying to offer to go inside with the boy and talk to the owner, she knew Collin was right. For once, she had to bite her tongue and let the cop do the talking.

Several long seconds passed while Mia thought she would burst. The need to blurt out reassurances and promises swelled like yeast bread on a hot day. Would Mitchell go on his own? Would Sergeant Grace drag him inside if he didn't?

As if in answer to her unasked question, Collin placed one wide hand on the knee of the boy's dirty blue jeans and patiently waited.

The gesture brought a lump to Mia's throat. Her brothers would laugh at her if they knew, but she couldn't help it. There was something moving about the sight of a tough, taciturn cop conveying his trustworthiness with a gentle touch.

The boy's shoulders were so tense, Mia thought his collarbone might snap. Finally, he drew in a shuddering breath and reached for his seat-belt clasp.

"Will you go with me?" Mouth tight and straight, he directed the question to Collin.

The policeman pushed to his feet. "Every step."

And then, as if the social worker in the front seat was invisible, the two males, one tall and buff and immaculate, the other small and thin and tattered, crossed the concrete space and went inside.

The kittens in the back seat made mewing sounds as Panda shifted positions. Mia glanced around to be sure they were staying put. Yellow eyes blinked back.

"Hang tight, Mama," she said. "The abandonment is only temporary."

The poor, bedraggled cat seemed satisfied to stay with her babies and the hapless turtle. So, Mia tilted her forehead against the cool side glass and watched the people inside the store. There were a few customers coming and going, an occasional car door slammed, though the area was reasonably quiet.

She could see Collin and Mitchell moving around inside, see the clerk. Although frustrated at being left behind, for once, she didn't charge into the situation. But she did use her time to pray that somehow the angry shop owner would give the child a break without letting him off scot-free.

Ten minutes later, Collin and Mitch emerged from the building. Collin wore his usual bland expression that gave nothing away. Mitch looked pale, but relieved as he slammed into the back seat.

Mia could hardly contain herself. "How did it go?"

"Okay." Collin started the cruiser and pulled into the lane of slow Sunday-afternoon traffic.

Mia rolled her eyes. That wasn't the answer she was asking for. But since the cop wasn't willing to elaborate, she asked Mitchell. "What was decided? Is he going to press charges?"

Mitch trailed a finger over one of the kittens. "I don't know yet. But he said he'd think about it."

The quiet, gentle boy she usually encountered had returned. The belligerence, most likely posturing brought on by fear, had dissipated. He looked young and small and lost.

Collin spoke up—finally. "We worked out a deal."

"And is this a secret all-male deal? Or can the nosy, female social worker be let in on it?"

Collin glanced her way, eyes sparkling. At least she'd badgered a smile out of him. Sort of.

"Didn't like being left in the car?"

The rat. He had already figured out that she needed to be in the middle of a situation. "This is the sort of thing I'm trained to do. I might have been useful in there."

He didn't argue the point. "We're asking for twenty hours of community service."

That was something she could help with.

"I'll talk to the DA if you'd like." She did that all the time, working deals for the juveniles she encountered. "He's a friend."

"Figures."

"Having friends is not a bad thing, Sergeant."

"It is when you use them to harass people."

Ah, the phone calls to the chief had not pleased him. "I did not harass you."

He lifted an eyebrow at her.

"Well, okay. Maybe I did. But just a little to get your attention."

"You got it."

"Was that a good thing or a bad thing?"

"Time will tell."

Was that a smile she saw? Or a grimace? He was the hardest man in the world to read.

The cruiser pulled to a stop in front of an older frame house in a rundown area of the city. Paint had peeled until the place was more gray than white, and the yard was overgrown. A rusted lawnmower with grass shooting up over the motor looked as though it hadn't been used all summer.

Mia knew the house. She'd been here more than once at the request of the school system, but never could find out anything that justified removing the boy from the home.

"I thought Mitch opted for Juvenile Hall?" she asked.

Collin shut off the engine and opened the car door. "He changed his mind."

A dark-haired woman who was far too thin came out into the yard and stood with her arms folded around her waist.

"Where's my ten bucks?" she asked as soon as Mitch was out of the car.

To Mia's surprise, Mitch reached in his jeans and withdrew a crumpled bill. She looked at Sergeant Grace, suspicious, but the man's poker face gave away nothing. The idea that the tough cop might have bailed the boy out with his mother touched her. Maybe he wasn't so heartless after all.

She listened without comment as Collin apprised Mitchell's mother about the situation. Mrs. Perez didn't seem too pleased with her son, as expected, but her fidgety behavior raised Mia's suspicions. She didn't invite them into the house and seemed anxious to have them gone.

"What's going to happen to him?" she asked. "I don't have no money for lawyers and courts."

"He broke the law, Mrs. Perez. Miss Carano will talk to the DA for him, but at the least he'll do some community service to pay for the things he took from the store."

"He stole from me, too."

Collin's nostrils flared. "You want to press charges?"

Said aloud, the idea seemed harsh even to the fidgety mother. "I don't want him stealing from me anymore. That's all. He'll end up in jail like his old man."

Conversation halted as an old car, the chassis nearly dragging on the street, mufflers missing or altered, rumbled slowly past. Loud hip-hop music pulsed from the interior, overriding every other sound.

Collin turned and stared hard-eyed at the vehicle, garnering a rude gesture in return. Mia had a feeling the car's inhabitants hadn't seen the last of Sergeant Grace.

When the racket subsided, Mia picked up the conversation. "Have you considered counseling?"

Monica Perez rolled her eyes. "Mitchell don't need no shrink. He needs a new set of friends. Them Walters boys down the street get into everything. You oughta go arrest them."

"I could help him meet some new friends if you'd

like," Mia said and received a sideways glance from Collin for her efforts.

"Fine with me."

"My church has a basketball league for kids. He could sign up to play."

"I wouldn't mind that, but I ain't got a car. Is it far from here?"

"I'll pick him up. Saturday morning at nine, if he wants to go." She looked at Mitch, stuck like a wood tick to Collin's side. "Mitch?"

"Sure. I guess so."

Collin dropped a hand on the boy's shoulder. "Miss Carano's going out on a limb for you."

Mitch gazed up at the tall cop, his expression a mix of frightened child and troubled youth. "I know."

Mia glimpsed his bewilderment, his failure to understand his own behavior. And as always, something about this kid got to her. A good person was inside there. With God's help, she'd find a way to bring him out.

"Someone will give you a call next week and let you know the DA's decision," Collin was telling Mrs. Perez.

And then with a curt nod, he turned and started back toward the police car. Mia, who preferred long goodbyes with lots of conversation and closure, felt off balance.

Mitch didn't seem to be finished either because he darted after the departing figure.

"Sergeant Grace."

Collin stopped, one hand on the car door.

Suddenly, every vestige of the tough street kid was gone. Mitch looked like what he was, a little boy with nothing and no one to cling to. "You'll take care of Panda?"

"I will."

"Can I come see her sometime?"

The hardened cop studied the small, intense face, his own face intense as if the answer would cost him too much. "She'd be sad if you didn't."

Mia said a quick goodbye to Mrs. Perez and hurried across the overgrown lawn. Now was her chance. Now that Collin had softened just the tiniest bit.

"I could bring Mitch out to your place. Anytime that's convenient for you."

Collin looked from Mitchell to Mia and back again. Mia was certain she must be imagining things because the strong, hardened cop looked more helpless than the boy. Helpless…and scared.

Mia shoved away from the mile-high stack of file folders on her desk and scrounged in the bottom desk drawer for her stash of miniature Snickers. A day like today required chocolate and plenty of it. She took two.

Her case load grew exponentially every day to the point that she was overwhelmed at times. Looking out for the interests of kids was her calling, but on days like today, the calling was a tough one.

She'd made a school visit and six home visits. At the last one, she'd done what every social worker dreads. She'd pulled the two neglected babies and taken them to a foster home. Even now, though she knew she'd made the right choice, she could hear the youngest one crying for his mama. Poor little guy was too young to comprehend that he lived in a crack house.

She nipped the corner of Snickers number one and turned to the computer on her desk. All the reports from today had to be typed up and stored in the master files before she could go home.

"See ya tomorrow, Mia," one of the other workers called as she passed by the open office door.

Mia waved without lifting her eyes from the computer screen. "Have a good evening, Allie."

She reached for another bite of candy. Over the tick-tick-tick of the keyboard, she heard another voice. This one wasn't her coworker.

"Mind if I interrupt for a minute?"

Her head snapped up.

"Collin?" she blurted before remembering he'd never given her permission to call him by his first name. But she had to face the fact. She thought about him, even prayed for him, by his first name.

During the three days since he'd helped her find Mitchell, she'd prayed about him and thought about him a lot. The fact that she didn't know him that well didn't get him out of her mind. She was intrigued.

And attracted. More than once, she'd wondered if he was a Christian, but she was afraid she might already know the answer.

Now he stood before her in his blue uniform, patches on each sleeve, shiny metal pins on each collar point and above his name tag. He looked as crisp and clean as new money.

Great. And she looked like a worn-out, overworked social worker whose white blouse was wrinkled and pulling loose from her red skirt. She hoped like crazy there was no chocolate on her teeth.

"Can we talk?"

Collin Grace wanted to talk? Now there was a novel concept.

"Do you know how?" She softened the teasing jab with a smile.

Those brown eyes twinkled but he didn't return the smile. "I want to make a deal with you."

He scraped a client chair away from her desk a little. He might want to talk, but he was still keeping his distance.

Mia rolled back in her own chair to study his solemn face. Whatever was on his mind was serious business. "A deal?"

"In exchange for your help, I'll mentor the kid."

The wonderful thrill of victory shot much-needed energy into her bloodstream. After the day she'd had, this was great news.

"Mitchell Perez? Collin, that's marvelous. He told

me on the phone last night that you stopped by after school yesterday. That was so nice of you, and it really made his day. He tried to act all tough about your visit, but he was thrilled. I could tell. And when I told him the DA agreed to community service, he asked if he could work for you. But I had no idea how to answer that without talking to you first and I've just been so busy today...."

Collin lifted one hand to slow her down. "The deal first."

Once she got on a roll, stopping was difficult. But that halted her in her tracks. "Am I going to like this deal?"

"This is confidential. Okay?"

Now her interest was piqued. Very. "Most of my work is confidential. Believe it or not, I can keep my mouth shut when necessary."

He made a huffing noise that sounded remarkably close to a laugh. She got up and moved around the desk past him to close the door even though the office was probably empty by now.

When she sat down again, she had to ask, "Do I have chocolate on my teeth?"

This time he *did* laugh.

"No. You look great."

"Such a smooth liar," she said, and then reached in the file drawer and took out another candy bar. "Want one?"

"No, thanks."

"Oh, yeah. You're the health-food cop. Poor guy. You don't know what you're missing." She unwrapped a Snickers, nibbled the end and shifted into social-worker mode.

"You said you needed my help. What can I do for you, Officer?"

"Collin's okay."

Another thrill, this one as sweet as the caramel, and completely uncalled for, raced through her. Before she could wipe the smile off her face, he did it for her.

"I want you to help me find my brothers."

She blinked, uncomprehending. "Your brothers?"

"Yeah." Collin leaned forward, muscled forearms on his thighs as he clasped his hands in front of him. Steel intensity radiated from him as though the coming confidence was very difficult for him to share. "My little brothers, Drew and Ian, though neither of them are little now."

She got a sinking feeling in the pit of her stomach. "When did you last see them?"

His answer hurt her heart. "More than twenty years ago."

"Tell me," she said simply, knowing for once when to keep quiet and let the other person do the talking. Whatever he had to share, in confidence, about his brothers was important to him.

Over the next fifteen minutes, during which Mia went through three more Snickers bars, Collin told a story all too familiar to a seasoned social worker. Oh, he spoke in vague, simplistic terms about his childhood, but Mia had worked in social services long enough to fill in the blanks. Collin and his brothers had been separated by the social system because of major issues in his family.

"What happened after that day in the principal's office? Where did you go? Foster care?" she asked, hearing the compassion in her voice and wondering if he would resent it. But she had brothers she adored, too. She knew how devastated she would be if she couldn't find one of them.

"Foster care never worked out for me. I went into a group home," he said simply, and she heard the hurt through the cold retelling. "Ian was so little, not even five. Foster care, maybe even adoption, would be my best guess for him. He was small and sweet and cute. He could have made the adjustment, I think." His nostrils flared. "I hope."

"And your middle brother? Drew? What do you think happened to him?"

He shook his head. The skin over his high, handsome cheekbones drew tight, casting deep hollows in his face. Clearly, talking about the loss of his brothers distressed him. "Drew was a fighter. He would have had a harder time than I did. I remember the social worker that day saying he was headed to a special place or something like that."

"A therapeutic home?"

"Maybe. I don't remember." He pinched at his upper lip, frustrated. "See? That's the problem. I was a kid, too. My memories are more feelings than facts."

And those feelings still cut into him with the power of a chainsaw.

"Did you ever see or hear anything at all about them? Anything that could help us find them?" She didn't know why she'd said *us*. She hadn't agreed to do anything yet.

"The summer after we were separated, we both ended up at one of those summer-camp things they do for kids in the system. We immediately started making plans to run away together. But, like I said, Drew was a fighter. He got kicked out the second day. I didn't even know about the trouble until he was gone."

"And no one told you anything about him?"

"No more than I've told you. Twenty years of searching, of sticking my name in files and on search boards and registries hasn't found them." The skin on his knuckles alternated white and brown as he flexed and unflexed his clenched fists. "I've had leads, good ones, but they were always dead ends."

And it's killing you. All the things she'd wondered about him now made sense. His chilly reserve. The way he seemed isolated, a man alone.

Collin Grace *had* been alone most of his life. He'd been a child alone. Now he was a man alone.

To a woman surrounded by the warmth and noise and love of a big family, Collin's situation was not only sad, it was tragic.

"Somewhere out there I have two brothers. I want them back." And then as if the words came out without his permission, he murmured gruffly, "I need to know they're okay."

Of course he needed that. Mia's training clicked through her head. As the oldest of the three boys, he'd been responsible for the others. Or at least, he'd thought he was. Having them taken away without a word left him believing he'd failed them.

Now she understood why he'd been so reluctant to take Mitchell under his wing. He was afraid of failing him, too.

The sudden insight almost brought tears to her eyes.

Mia tilted back her chair and drew in a breath, studying the poster on the far wall. The slogan, Social Work Is Love Made Visible, reminded her why she did what she did. The love of Christ in her, and through her, ministered to people like Collin, to kids like Mitchell. If she could help, she would.

"Twenty years is forever in the social services system. Do you really think I can find them if you haven't had any success?"

"You know the system better than I do. You have access to records that I don't even know exist. Records that I'm not allowed to see."

Warning hackles rose on Mia's back. She tried not

to let them show. “You aren’t asking me to go into sealed records without permission, are you?”

“Would you?” Dark eyes studied her. He wasn’t pressing, just asking.

“No.” She’d done that once for her oldest brother, Gabe. The favor had cost her a job she loved and a certain amount of credibility with her peers. The bad decision had also cost her a great deal emotionally and spiritually. God had forgiven her, but she’d always felt as if she’d let Him down. “I will never compromise my professional or my Christian ethics.”

Again.

“Okay, then. Do what you can. You still have access to a lot of records, even the unsealed ones. I’ve looked everywhere I know, but that’s the problem. I don’t know how to navigate the system the way you would. I can’t seem to find much when it comes to child welfare records of twenty years ago.”

“Records from back then aren’t computerized.”

“I finally figured that one out. But where are they?”

“If they exist, they’re still in file cabinets somewhere or they could be piled in boxes in a storage warehouse.”

“Like police records.”

“Exactly.” She crumpled the half-dozen Snickers wrappers into a wad, dismayed to have consumed so many.

“Are you willing to try?”

“Are you willing to be Mitchell’s CAP? That’s

what we call adults who volunteer through our Child Advocate Partners Program." She would help Collin in his search no matter what, but Mitch might as well get a good mentor out of the deal.

"What do I have to do?"

"Some initial paperwork. Being a police officer simplifies the procedure since you already have clearances."

"How much is the welfare office involved?"

"You don't like us much, do you?"

He made a face that said he had good reason.

"Things are different now, Collin. We understand things about children today that we didn't know then."

He didn't buy a word of it. "Yeah. Well."

"If I help you and you become Mitch's CAP, you're going to be stuck with me probably more than you want to be."

"As long as it's you. And only you."

Now why did that make her feel so good? "But you think I talk too much."

The corner of his mouth hiked up. "You do."

"But you're willing to sacrifice?"

"Finding my brothers is worth anything."

Ouch. "Sorry. I was teasing, but maybe I shouldn't have. Finding your brothers *is* serious business."

"No apology necessary." He rose with athletic ease, bringing with him the vague scent of woodsy cologne and starched uniform. "I was teasing, too."

He was? Nice to know he could. "I'll need all the

information you can give me about your brothers. Ages, names, dates you can remember, people you remember, places. Any little detail."

From his shirt pocket, he withdrew a small spiral notebook, the kind all cops seemed to carry. "The basics are in here. But I have more information on my computer."

"What kind of information?"

"The research I've done. Names and places I've already eliminated. Group homes, foster parents. I know a lot of places my brothers never were. I just can't find where they are."

He made the admission easily, but Mia read the hopelessness behind such a long and fruitless search. Twenty years was a long time to keep at it. But Collin Grace didn't seem the kind that would ever give up.

And that was exactly the type of person she was, too.

"Everything you've investigated will be useful. Knowing where *not* to look is just as important as knowing where *to* look. The files and the computer will be helpful, but we may have to do some legwork as well." Now, why did the prospect of going somewhere with Collin sound so very, very appealing? "People are more comfortable with face-to-face questions about these kinds of things."

"Whatever it takes."

"I can't make promises, but I'll do what I can."

"Fair enough."

"Then I guess we have a deal. Will you go out and talk to Mitchell or do you want me to?"

Reluctance radiated from him in waves, but he'd made a deal and he was the kind of man who would keep it. Wasn't he still trying to keep a promise he'd made when he was ten years old? A man like that didn't back off from responsibility.

"I can contact him tomorrow," she offered.

"We could both tell him now. You know what's involved more than I do."

She shook her head, more disappointed than was wise, considering how little she knew about Collin as a person.

"I'm slammed with extra work tonight. I'll be here until seven at least." And Mitch was a lot more interested in Collin that he was in Mia.

"Too bad," he said. His expression was unreadable as usual so Mia didn't know what to make of his comment. Too bad she couldn't go with him? Or too bad she had so much work to do?

Either way, she watched him turn and stride out of her office and suffered a twinge of regret that she hadn't gone along anyway. She could be dishonest and say she wanted another look at Mitchell's living situation or that she needed to explain the program in more detail. But Mia was not dishonest. Even with herself. She had wanted to spend time with her enigmatic policeman.

And the notion was disturbing to say the least. She

hadn't dated anyone in a while. To find her interest piqued by a man who didn't even seem to like her was a real puzzle.

He was a good cop, had a good reputation, and she'd had a sneak peek at the kindness he kept safely hidden. But he also carried a personal history that sometimes meant major emotional issues. Issues that might require counseling and work and, most importantly, healing from God.

And that was the big issue for Mia. Was Collin Grace a believer?

She reached for another Snickers.

# *Chapter Five*

Sometimes Collin felt as if he spent his life inside a vehicle. He'd driven from Mia's office directly to Mitch's place, only to find the little twerp wasn't there. After driving through the neighborhood, he'd spotted him in a park shooting hoops with three other boys.

When Collin got out of the cruiser, Mitchell passed the ball off and headed toward him. The other boys quickly faded into the twilight and disappeared.

"Why are your friends in such a rush?" Collin leaned against the side of the car and folded his arms, watching the shadowy figures with a mixture of amusement and suspicion.

"You scared them off."

"They have reason to be scared of a cop?"

"Maybe."

Which meant yes in eleven-year-old talk.

"It's getting dark. Come on. I'll take you home."

"Am I in trouble?" Mitch asked, climbing readily into the front seat of the cruiser.

"No more than usual."

Streetlights had come on but made little dent in the shadowy time between day and night. This part of town was a haven for the unsavory. Gang types, thugs, druggies, thieves all came sneaking out like cockroaches as soon as the sun went down. No place at all for a young boy.

Collin had to admit Mia was right about one thing. This kid needed a mentor before he fell into the cesspool that surrounded him. Though he still wasn't sure he wanted to be the one, Collin had begun to feel a certain responsibility toward Mitchell. He hated that, but he did. Who better than him to understand what this kid was going through? And that was all he planned to do. Understand and guide. He wasn't letting the kid get to him.

"Why're you here?" Mitch slouched down into the seat and stared out the window at the passing cars with studied disinterest.

"Miss Carano sent me."

Mitch sat up. "No kidding? You gonna be my CAP?"

So, she'd already prepared the kid for this. How had she known he would agree? He hadn't even known himself.

"What do you think about that?"

The kid hitched a shoulder. "I got plenty of other stuff to do."

"Yeah. Including a lot of community service. At least ten hours at the store where you jacked the stuff. The rest is up to you and me and Miss Carano."

"I guess I could come out to your place. Help with the animals. I'm good at that."

"Up to you." Mitch had to make the decision. Otherwise, he'd only resent Collin's interference.

"Panda probably misses me a lot. She doesn't trust many people."

"With good reason." A lot of people had let the cat—and the kid—down. The cruiser eased to a stop at the light. "You work for me, you'll have to lose the cigarettes."

The denial came fast. "I don't smoke."

One hand draped over the steering wheel, Collin just looked at him, long and steady. The boy's eyes shifted sideways. He swallowed and hitched a shoulder. "How'd you know?"

"I have a nose." The light changed. "Gonna lose them or not?"

"Whatever."

"Your choice."

"Why do you care?"

"The animals at my place depend on me."

"What's that got to do with anything?"

"You think about it and let me know which is more important. The animals or the smokes."

Collin slowed and turned into the drive-through of a Mickey D's. "Want a burger?"

He rolled down his window. The smell of hot vegetable oil surrounded the place.

"Miss Carano said you didn't eat junk food."

"She did?" The fact that she'd mentioned him to the boy in any way other than as a court-appointed advocate sent a warm feeling through him. Warm, like her sunny smile.

That warmth, that genuine caring both drew and repelled him. He didn't understand it. But he couldn't deny how good it had felt to dump his burden on her desk and to believe she would do exactly what she promised. Maybe she'd have no better luck than he'd had in finding Drew and Ian. But for the first time in years, he felt renewed hope.

Hanging out with a social worker might not be so bad after all.

Little more than a week later, Collin considered changing his mind.

He stood in the last stall of his barn showing Mitchell how to measure horse feed. The smell of hay and horses circled around his head.

The kid was all right most of the time. The social worker was a different matter.

He did okay on the days Mia dropped Mitch off as planned, said hello and goodbye and drove away in her power suit and speedy little yellow Mustang. The days she climbed out of that Mustang wearing blue jeans and a T-shirt gave him trouble. Regardless that she was here on business to assess the CAP arrangement, dressed like that, she was a woman, not a social worker. It was hard to dislike one and like the other, so he tried to keep his distance.

Trouble was, Mia didn't understand the concept of personal space. She was in his, talking a mile a minute, smile warm, attitude sweet. The more he retreated, the more she advanced.

Over the clatter of horse pellets hitting metal, he could hear her talking in soft, soothing tones to Happy, the pup with the lousy luck and the cheerful outlook.

"How much feed does Smokey get?" Mitch's question pulled Collin back to the horse feed.

"None of the pellets. Just some of this alfalfa."

Mitch frowned, dubious. "He's awful skinny."

"Too much at first can kill him."

"How come somebody let him get like that? I can see his ribs."

The buckskin colt stood quivering in the stall, head down, so depressed Collin wondered if he'd survive.

"Some people don't care."

It was a cold, hard fact that both he and the boy knew all too well. "Yeah."

In the few days Mitch had been here, Collin had ferreted out a few unsavory facts about his home life. The stepdad wasn't exactly father-of-the-year material. And mom wouldn't win any prizes either, although the kid was loyal to her anyway. Collin didn't press him about his mother. He'd been the same once, until the woman who'd birthed him walked away and never looked back. He hoped that never happened to Mitchell.

Hand full of green, scented hay, the kid knelt in front of the little horse. "Come on, Smokey. It's okay."

The colt nuzzled the outstretched fingers, then nibbled a bit of grass.

Mitch had a way with all the creatures on the farm. Even Doc had commented on that. Like a magnet, he was drawn to the sickest ones, the most wounded, the near-hopeless. Street-kid wariness melted into incredible tenderness when he approached the animals. Not one of them shied away from the boy's tenacious determination to make them all well.

"I promised Happy I'd soak his foot later. Is that okay?" Mitchell was on a mission to save the crippled little collie. Every day, he went to Happy's stall first and last with some extra time in between.

"What did Doc say?"

"She said extra soaks can't hurt nothing."

She was right about that. Happy's foot had reached the point when hope was all but gone. Soaking couldn't make the wound any worse, and any action at all made them feel as if they were doing something. "All right then."

Collin moved down the corridor, taking care of the menial tasks so necessary for the survival of these wounded creatures who depended on him. Cleaning pens, scooping waste, lining stalls and boxes with fresh straw.

Mia was inside the cat pen.

He frowned at her. “I thought you left.” He hadn’t really, but he didn’t know what else to say.

“You wish.” With a laugh, she lifted one of Panda’s kittens from the box and draped the fur ball over her shoulder. “What’s wrong? Rough day?”

Yeah, he’d had a lousy day, but how did she know? He didn’t like having some woman, a social worker at that, inside his head.

“I’m all right.” He ducked into Happy’s stall to escape her. She followed, but didn’t press him about his gray mood.

“Mitch seems to be doing a good job for you, don’t you agree?”

“Yeah.” The dog wobbled up from his straw bed, tail wagging. The smell of antiseptic and dying flesh was hard to ignore.

“Has he opened up at all about why he runs away so much?”

“A little.”

“But you’re not going to tell me.”

“Confidential.”

She rolled her big eyes at him. She had interesting eyes. Huge and almond-shaped, soft and sparkly. He didn’t know how a person made her eyes sparkly, but she did.

Mia knelt to stroke the pup while still holding the

kitten against her shoulder. Happy, tail thumping a mile a minute, didn't seem to mind having a cat invade his territory. Dumb dog didn't seem to mind much of anything.

"What's going to happen to him?"

"Happy? Or Mitch?"

She gave him another of her wide-eyed looks. He wanted to laugh. "The dog."

"If things don't improve this week, Doc's going to amputate the other foot on Monday."

"Oh, Collin." Her face was stricken. She glanced toward the stall door. "Does Mitch know?"

"No."

"No wonder you're in a bad mood tonight. I thought maybe you'd had to shoot somebody today."

"That would have made me feel better."

She looked up. "Not funny."

"Sorry. Bad cop joke." Using force was the last thing he ever wanted.

"How do you cops do that, anyway? Shoot somebody, I mean."

"We pretend they're lawyers." He shook kibble into Happy's bowl. "Or social workers."

"Ha-ha. I'm laughing." But she did giggle. "When are you going to tell him?"

He crumpled an empty feed sack into an oversize ball. "I don't know."

"Want me to do it?"

"My responsibility." He tossed the sack into a

trash bin and knelt beside the pup. "I wish I knew who did this to him."

The little dog licked his outstretched hand, liquid brown eyes delighted by the attention. Anger and helplessness pushed inside Collin's chest. He hated feeling helpless.

"I ran a computer search of the system today on you and your brothers."

His pulse quickened though he told himself to expect nothing. "And came up empty?"

"Mostly."

"Figures." Refusing to be disappointed, he stood and took the kitten from her. The soft, warm body wiggled in protest. As many years as he'd searched he couldn't expect miracles from Mia in a week.

"There's some information about you, but the facts on Drew and Ian seem to be the same that you already have. A couple of foster placements. Some medical records."

He wanted to ask what she'd found on him, but didn't bother. She'd probably tell him anyway. Mia already knew too much about him and she was likely to learn more. Opening his sordid background to anyone always made him feel vulnerable, and nothing scared him like vulnerability.

He led the way out of Happy's stall to take the kitten back to Panda. A glance toward the horses told him Mitch was busy mucking out stalls. A perverse part of him figured that particular job was adequate punishment for shoplifting.

"Collin."

He lowered the tiny tabby to her mother. Panda's burns were healing, but she didn't let anyone except Mitch touch her. Even Doc had had to sedate the cat before treating the wounds, an unusual turn of events.

"Collin," she said again, this time from beneath his elbow.

With a sigh, he turned. "What?"

She wrinkled her nose at him, fully aware her chatter bothered him. She looked cute, and he didn't like it. Social workers weren't supposed to be cute.

"I brought the file of information with me. Do you want to see it?"

"Might as well."

Nothing like cold, hard welfare facts to make a man stop thinking about a pretty woman.

Inside Collin's house for the first time, Mia thought the interior of the unfinished, basically unfurnished house was exactly what she expected of him. Neat and tidy to a fault, one long room served as kitchen, living room, and dining room. The furniture consisted of an easy chair, a TV and a small dining-room set. There were no pictures on the walls, no curtains on the shaded windows, no plants or other decorating touches. Collin lived a neatly Spartan lifestyle.

To Mia, who lived in a veritable jungle of plants, terra-cotta pots and pieces of Tuscan decor jammed into a tiny apartment, the house was sadly bare but filled with potential. A pot here. A plant there.

"I live simply," he said when he caught her looking.

"The place has great potential."

"It's not even finished."

"That's why it has great potential."

He shook his head and pulled out two chairs. "Sit. I'll move the laptop."

She eyed the animated screen saver. "Did Mitchell do that?"

"Yeah. He loves the thing."

Mia knew the boy didn't have a computer at home. "His teacher says he's a regular whiz kid."

"He knows keystroke shortcuts I didn't know existed and can navigate sites I can't get into. I'm afraid to ask if he's ever tried hacking."

"The answer is probably yes."

"I know." With a self-deprecating laugh that surprised her, Collin admitted, "He even offered to teach me keyboarding."

"You should let him. Teaching you would be good for his self-esteem."

"It wouldn't be too good for mine." He wiggled his two index fingers. "Old habits die hard."

A large brown envelope lay on the table beside the computer. She reached for it. "Is that more information about your brothers?"

"No. Just another problem I'm working on."

"Anything I can help with?"

"Not unless you're a lawyer. My neighbor," he said, his lips twisted, "is suing me."

"What for?" She couldn't imagine Collin Grace ever being intrusive enough for any neighbor even to know him, much less be at cross-purposes.

"He claims one of my animals has attacked his prize sheep on more than one occasion."

"They couldn't." All the animals here were both too sick and too well-confined to bother anything.

"Cecil Slokum has found something to complain about ever since I bought this place."

"Why?"

"Don't know. This time though," he waved the envelope in the air, "I ran a background check on him."

"Oooh, suspicious. Remind me never to tick you off."

"Too late."

There was that wicked sense of humor again, coming out of nowhere.

"Have you hired an attorney?"

"No."

"You should."

"And I suppose you just happen to know one. Or two. Maybe you even know the judge."

"Well..." She cupped her hands under her chin and leaned toward him. "As a matter of fact, one of my brothers is an attorney. He's also a city councilman."

Collin leaned back his chair. "So he's the one."

"Don't look like that. If my brother hadn't spoken to the chief, you might never have agreed to mentor Mitch. And you like having him out here. You know you do."

"The kid's all right. He's good for the animals."

She laughed. If Collin wanted to pretend he cared nothing about the boy, fine. But he did.

"You've made more progress with Mitchell in a week than anyone else has made in a year."

The boy basked in the policeman's attention, eager to please him, ready to listen to his few, terse words. According to his fifth-grade teacher, Mitch had even turned in all his homework this week, a first.

Collin set the laptop and the brown envelope on an empty chair. "So, you gonna show me that file you brought or talk me to death?"

"Both." She handed over the manila folder.

His eyes twinkled. "Figures."

"You won't die from a little conversation, Collin. Talking things out might do you some good."

She liked listening to his quiet, manly voice as much as she enjoyed looking at him. He was an attractive man. Mia squelched a stomach flutter. Very attractive.

Less intimidating in street attire, tonight he wore a Tac-team T-shirt neatly tucked into well-worn blue jeans. Muscular biceps, fine-cut by exercise and work, stretched the sleeves snug.

"I keep noticing your tattoo." Among other things. "What is it?"

He looked up from studying the file. For a moment, she thought he wouldn't tell her, but then he pushed the sleeve higher and rotated toward her.

Her heart stutter-stepped. Each leaf of a small shamrock bore, not initials as she'd thought, but a name. "Drew, Ian, Collin," she read.

"I didn't want to forget," he said simply. "Not even for a day."

All her preconceived ideas about tattoos went flying out the door. Without forethought, Mia placed her fingers on his arm just beneath the clover. His dark skin was warm and firm and strong with leashed power.

"What an incredibly loving thing to do."

He slid away from her and stood, closing the file. "Mitch should be up here by now. He has homework."

Helping Mitchell with his homework hadn't been part of the court order but Collin didn't let that deter him.

He crossed the few steps to the door and stood gazing out, his back to her. She felt the uncertainty in him, the discomfort that she'd generated with her comment. Or maybe with her touch. One thing was clear. Collin had a hard time expressing emotions. He might feel them. He just couldn't let them show.

She held back a smile. To an Italian, Collin Grace was a red flag waved in front of a bull. Expression was what she and her family did best. She would either drive Collin crazy or help him heal. She hoped it was the latter. Collin had a lot to offer people if he would only open up and trust a little more.

"Collin?"

He tensed but didn't turn around. "What?"

"My family's having a birthday party on Saturday for Nic, my youngest brother. He's turning twenty-one. If you'll come, I'll introduce you to Adam. He might be able to help with the lawsuit."

He looked at her over one shoulder. "How many brothers do you have?"

"Three bros, one sister and a lot of cousins, aunts and uncles."

"You're lucky."

"Yes. Incredibly blessed. You'll like them, Collin. They're great people."

He turned all the way around, tilting his head so she would know he teased. "Do they all talk as much as you?"

She grinned. "All but Uncle Vitorio. Come on, Collin. Say you'll be there."

"I wouldn't want to intrude." Which meant he wanted to come.

"No such thing at a Carano gathering. We have a motto. The more the merrier."

"Not too original."

She shrugged. "Who cares? It fits. So what do you say?" She really, really wanted him to come. For professional reasons, of course.

Cocoa-colored eyes holding hers, he considered the invitation for a minute but finally said, "Better not."

Disappointment seeped into her, but disappeared as quickly as the next thought arrived. "You could bring Mitch. He needs to interact with a strong family unit, and even if I do say so myself, mine fits the bill."

Hanging out with the Caranos would be good for Collin, too, but she couldn't say that.

"Proud of them, are you?"

"They're a little crazy, and none of us is perfect by any stretch of the imagination, but yeah, I have a great family."

"Taking Mitch is a good idea, but you don't need me along."

"He won't go without you." And she was glad. Collin needed the warm circle of family around him as much as the child did. A man who'd grown up in the system wouldn't have had too many opportunities to witness healthy family relationships. Besides, the Caranos were a lot of fun and if anyone could melt the ice shield from Collin and Mitchell, her family could.

"Here he comes now," she said at the sound of feet tromping on the porch. "Why don't we ask him?"

Collin held the door open as Mitch, Archie the turtle in hand, came inside. To everyone's astonishment, the turtle with the cracked shell was thriving.

"Ask me what?" The little turtle's claws scratched at the air and found purchase when Mitchell placed him on the table.

"You want to go to a party at my house on Saturday?"

Mitch squinted at Mia and then up at Collin. "You going?"

Mia giggled. Collin slanted his eyes at her in silent warning. She laughed out loud.

"It'll be a great party. Lots of food and games and craziness. My folks have a swimming pool." She let that little bit of enticement dangle.

Scooping Archie against his chest, Mitch plopped into a chair. "A real pool? Or one of them kiddie things?"

"Above-ground, but it's big. Has a slide and everything."

"Are your parents rich?"

Mia laughed. "No. They've run a little family bakery forever, but they know how to save money for the things that matter."

Mitch eyeballed Collin, who had gone to the fridge for boxes of juice. Mia knew avoidance behaviors when she saw them.

"They probably wouldn't want me to come." The boy's voice held a longing that neither adult could miss. "I don't have any trunks."

Collin slammed a straw through the top of a juice box with such force the plastic bent.

"We'll get some," he said gruffly.

"You're going too?" Mitch sat up straight and punched the air. "All right. This will be awesome!"

Collin sent Mia a look that would have quelled anyone but a determined social worker.

And she knew she'd won.

## Chapter Six

By the time Saturday afternoon rolled around, the knot in Collin's stomach had grown from the size of a pea to that of a watermelon. Mitchell wasn't in any better shape. The kid, usually mouthy as Mia, had barely said two words on the drive to the Carano place.

Collin knew how the kid felt. Out of place. A misfit. The uncertainty was one of the reasons he avoided hanging out with his police buddy, Maurice. How did a person fit into a family when they didn't know what a family should be?

But Collin had learned about and yearned for the kind of relationships Mia bragged about. Even if he might never have them for himself, he wanted them for Mitch. The kid needed to know there was better out there than a stepdad who knocked your mom around and hung out with thugs. Mitchell needed this, which was exactly why Collin had swallowed his reluctance and put on a show about wanting to meet the Caranos.

When they pulled up in front of the sprawling home in a nice older neighborhood in northwest Oklahoma City, a half-dozen other cars already lined the street out front. Collin did his usual scan of the premises, committing the vehicle descriptions and the entrances and exits to memory, the police officer in him never off duty.

Mitch fidgeted with his seat belt. "You think they'll like me?"

The question bothered Collin but he didn't let his feelings show. The kid already knew that people would judge him by his rough clothes and poor grammar. He might as well have White Trash tattooed on his forehead.

"If Mia likes you, they will, too."

"She likes me because she has to. It's her job."

Collin squeezed the back of Mitch's neck. "You know better."

"Yeah." The boy pumped his eyebrows in silliness. "She likes me 'cause I'm cute."

Collin made a rude noise. Mitch's laughter relaxed them both.

As they started up the hedge-lined walkway, squeals and laughter echoed from the backyard. A football came flying over a wooden privacy fence and landed at Collin's feet. He picked it up just as the gate opened. He expected a kid to come charging after the ball. Instead, a grown man, probably near his age, trotted toward him. His maroon T-shirt was sweat-plastered to his upper body.

Collin held up the ball. "This belong to you?"

"Coulda had a touchdown if I'd been taller." The man stopped in front of them and bent forward, hands on knees to catch his breath. "You must be Collin and Mitch. Glad you're here. Mia's wearing a hole in the carpet."

She was?

"I'm Adam, Mia's favorite brother." He laughed, smile bright in a dark face, and extended his hand to Mitch and then to Collin. "You must be the cop Mia's been telling us about."

She talked about him? "I hope it's good."

"So far."

The man was friendly enough, but Collin knew when he was being checked out. He didn't miss the subtle warning. Mess with a Carano and you have to answer to the whole clan. He admired that. He had been that way with his own brothers, though he was surprised that Adam would feel the need to warn him about anything. He'd come here to help a troubled kid, not because of Mia.

Adam tossed the ball back and forth from one hand to the other. "You play football?" he said to Mitchell.

"I stink at it."

"Awesome." Adam gently shoved the ball into the

boy's mid-section. "You can be on my team. We all stink at it, too. How about you, Collin?"

"Yeah. I stink at it, too."

Adam laughed and slapped him on the back. "Come on. I'll take you inside to find Mia. We'll get a game going later."

Adam's friendly greeting took some of the tension out of Collin's jaw. Maybe he could get through this afternoon with a minimum amount of stress.

Collin's first impression of the Carano house was the noise, good noise that came from talk and laughter and activity. Several conversations bounced around the large, crowded living room in competition with a big-screen TV blasting a game between the Texas Longhorns and the Oklahoma State Cowboys. There were kitchen noises too, of pots and pans and cabinets opening and closing.

Through patio doors at the opposite end, the pool was visible, along with the remnants of the touch football game they'd interrupted. He glanced down at Mitch, saw the boy scanning the backyard with typical kid radar. He figured Mitch would be fine as soon as he worked his way outside.

The incredible smell of home-cooked food issued from the enormous area to his left. The kitchen was exactly the kind he had envisioned for Mia, though she no longer lived here. Washed warm with sunlight and the rich earthy colors of brick-red flooring, the room was dappled with overflowing fruit baskets, clear jars of colorful pasta, and copper pots dangling above a center island. He located Mia at the island arranging cheese and fruit on a platter.

The knot in his stomach reacted oddly. He was glad to see her, whether because she was the only familiar face in the crowd or otherwise, he didn't know. And he wasn't bothering to go there. Two weeks ago, she was a pain in his neck.

She looked so natural here, so much more real than she did in her office and business suits. Home was her element.

She said something to a pretty older woman who could only be her mother. They both had the same large, almond eyes and full mouths. And like her mother, Mia tended to be more rounded and womanly than was currently the trend—a look Collin appreciated.

Today her long hair was down, flowing in soft red-brown waves around her shoulders. Her red T-shirt fitted her to perfection and topped off a pair of white, loose-fitting cropped pants and sandals.

She was talking—no big surprise—as she popped a piece of cheese in her mouth. Suddenly she laughed, clapping one hand over her lips.

"Hey Mia," Adam hollered over the noise. "You got company."

When she caught sight of him, her face brightened. Hurriedly, she said something over her shoulder, wiped her hands on a towel and rushed in their direction.

"You're here!" For a minute, Collin thought she might hug him. Instead, she grabbed his elbow with one hand, dropped the other arm over Mitch's shoulder, and drew them into the melee.

"I see you've already met Adam, so follow me and we'll try to forge a path to the others."

Adam disappeared into the mix as Mia introduced the newcomers to her sister, parents, grandparents and a number of other people whose connection escaped him.

"I don't expect you to remember everyone the first time," Mia said.

The first time? Collin wasn't sure he could survive a second go-round. Though everyone was as friendly as Mia, he felt like a bug under a microscope.

"This is my baby brother, Nic," Mia was saying. "The birthday boy."

"That's birthday *man* to you, big sister." Across Nic's T-shirt were the words, *What if the Hokey Pokey really* is *what it's all about?*

Mia laughed and rolled her eyes. "He's twenty-one today and I suspect he will be impossible to live with now that he thinks he's become one of the grown-ups."

Collin shook the younger man's hand. "Good to meet you, Nic. Happy birthday."

"Thanks," Nic answered, his grin wide as he looked from Collin to Mia. Speculation, totally unwarranted, was rife. Just what exactly had Mia told them about him anyway? "You want to hear some secrets about my evil big sister?"

Mia poked a teasing finger in Nic's chest. "No he doesn't. Not if you want to live to be twenty-two."

Speculation or not, Collin enjoyed the joking exchange between brother and sister.

He leaned toward Nic and spoke in a low voice. "Maybe we should talk later. When Mia isn't around."

Mia pretended horror. "Don't you dare. Nic tells lies about how mean I was to him when he was small."

"They're not lies. Just ask Adam." Nic whipped around. "Hey, Adam. Come help me out."

Adam, the football player in the maroon shirt, popped up from the couch where he was surrounded by kids who fell away like brushed-off dust. Collin was startled to see Mitchell in the mix. At some point the kid had wandered off toward the big-screen TV, and Collin hadn't even noticed. Chalk up one demerit for the Big Brother.

"What's up?" Adam asked, his sweaty T-shirt still damp and dark. "The birthday boy already showing off?"

"Of course," Mia said. "I'm leaving Collin in your mature company so I can help Mom and Grandma get dinner on the table. Do not allow Nic to tell horror stories."

Nic guffawed and Adam struggled to keep a straight face. "Sure, sis. Whatever you say."

"I mean it," she warned with a wagging finger. "Collin, I'll be back to rescue you in five minutes."

Then she returned to the oregano-scented kitchen, leaving Collin with Adam again. The feeling of abandonment came with startling swiftness, that emptiness he despised. Collin bit down on his back teeth, annoyed. He was a grown-up. He didn't need a babysitter. In fact, he didn't need to be here. He didn't fit.

He shifted uncomfortably and wished for a quiet corner where he could watch and listen without being noticed. Mitchell was probably miserable, too. But one look in the living room told him he was wrong. Mitch was deep in conversation with Mr. Carano and they were both fiddling with a laptop chess game. Give the kid a computer and he was at home anywhere. Collin envied that ease and wondered if he'd ever had it as a kid. If he had, it had been very early in his life. He sure didn't remember.

"You have that shell-shocked look that says Mia didn't warn you about us." Adam's voice broke into his thoughts.

"What? Sorry, my mind strayed."

"No wonder. The noise level in here could rival a landing strip."

"No problem." The noise wasn't what bothered him, though it *was* loud. Loud and enthusiastic. He could see where Mia got her positive energy and upbeat attitude.

"From the look on your face, I'd say your family isn't as big or rowdy as the Carano bunch."

"You'd be right about that." If he had a family.

Adam grabbed a bowl of chips from the coffee table. "Come on, let's head out to the backyard where there's some relative peace. There could be a football game in your future. How about you, Nic? Ready to rumble?"

"Not now. Dana Rozier just pulled up out front with a carload of babes." He cranked his eyebrows up and down a few times. "Can't disappoint the ladies."

Nic rubbed his hands together and then bounded for the front door.

"Ask them if they want to play football," Adam called and was rewarded with a hyena laugh from the birthday boy. "Oh, well, it was worth a try." He shook his head. "Nic and his girls. I don't see the attraction, do you?"

The Carano brothers were fun. He'd say that for them.

Adam shrugged, hollered at Gabe to organize a team, and then led the way through the sea of people and at least one large dog. The backyard was filled with kids, some swimming, two shooting hoops, and a couple of little ones just running in circles squealing for the joy of it.

Adam set the bowl of chips on the ground and collapsed into a lawn chair. "Grab a chair."

Collin did.

"Man, is this a gorgeous day or what?"

"Yeah." He thought of all the work he could be

doing on his house on a day like this. Winter would come soon and he wouldn't be any closer to finishing than he'd been at the beginning of summer.

"Mia says you run a rescue ranch for hurt animals."

"That's right."

"She told me about your problem."

Collin stiffened. Mia had promised to keep his search for Drew and Ian confidential. "Why would she do that?"

"Mia doesn't keep much from her family. But in this case she thought I could help."

He should have known he couldn't trust a social worker. "I can handle it."

"Sometimes lawsuits, even frivolous ones, can be tricky."

A truckload of tension rushed out of Collin. The lawsuit.

"Mia told me her brother was a lawyer. I didn't realize she meant you."

"I hope you didn't think she meant Nic."

They both chuckled. "Seeing him in a courtroom might be entertaining."

"What about in the operating room?"

"Excuse me?"

"He's applying for medical school. There really is a brain beneath that happy-go-lucky personality."

"I'm impressed."

"Don't be. He hasn't been accepted yet." Adam reached for another handful of tortilla chips and offered the bowl to Collin. "So how can I help you with this lawsuit?"

"I don't want to impose."

"No imposition. A friend of Mia's is a friend of mine."

Were they friends? He hadn't wanted to be, hadn't really thought about it until now. "She's a nice girl."

"A very nice girl." Adam shifted around in the lawn chair so they were face-to-face.

"Sometimes she pushes too hard, comes on too strong, but don't hold that against her. Gabe and I call her a coconut. Tough on the outside, a little nutty when she gets on one of her crusades to change the world, but soft and sweet on the inside."

Collin had seen the sweet side at the ranch. He'd also wrestled with her talkative, pushy side.

"She hounded me for days until I agreed to mentor Mitchell."

"See what I mean? She's so sure she can change the world with love and faith that she never gives up. Sometimes she gets hurt in the process. I wouldn't want to see that happen again."

Mia had been hurt? How? Why? And, most importantly, by whom? Collin, who seldom ate chips, took a handful.

"She's in a tough profession," was all he could think of. "The ugliness burns out a lot of strong people."

"Not Mia. She'll never let that happen. There's too much of God in her. She'll always stay tender and vulnerable to hurt. That's just the way she's made." Adam tossed a chip into the air, caught it in his mouth and crunched. "You know why she's not married?"

He'd wondered. Mia was smart, pretty, personable...though he wondered more that Adam would bring up the subject with a stranger like him. "I figure she's had her chances."

"She has. But Mia is waiting for the right guy. Not just any guy, but the one God sends."

Well, that left him out for sure. Not that it mattered. He wasn't in the market for a woman. Especially a nosey social worker who talked too much and made him think about things and feel things he'd kept buried most of his life.

Adam could relax. Neither he nor his sister had anything to fear from Collin Grace.

# *Chapter Seven*

"He's out in the backyard." Adam jerked a thumb in that direction. "The guy looked like he could use a breather from all of us."

Mia took a fresh glass of tea, sugarless the way she'd seen Collin take it during the meal, and pushed open the patio doors.

The glorious blue sky hung over a perfect early-autumn afternoon. She breathed in a happy breath of fresh air. What a great day this had been. Collin and Mitchell had seemed to have a good time. And her family had risen to the occasion as they always did, wrapping the two newcomers in a welcome of genuine friendliness. Nic had been his usual wild and crazy self, celebrating his twenty-first birthday by shooting videos of all the attendees wearing the Groucho glasses he'd bought for party favors.

This kind of gathering was good for Mitchell. He could learn here, interact with real men and motherly women, learn how to have fun in a clean and healthy way. Though she knew Collin would argue the fact, he needed this kind of thing, too. The protective shell around him kept away hurt, but it also kept away the good emotions.

When he'd walked in the door this afternoon, she'd been almost giddy with pleasure. Later, she'd have to examine that reaction.

In the shady overhang of the house, he leaned against the sun-warmed siding to watch Mitchell splash around in the pool. Was it her imagination or did Collin look isolated, maybe even lonely, standing there apart from the bustle of people? She'd thought a lot about him lately, about his upbringing, about how awful he must feel to be alone in the world, not knowing where his family was, or even if they were alive.

Yes, he was on her mind a great deal.

"You look like you could use this." Ice tinkled against the glass as she held the tea out to him.

"Thanks."

Mia wiped her hand, damp from condensation, down her pant leg. "Overwhelmed?"

He sipped at the tea and swallowed before answering. "A little."

"If a person survives their first dose of Caranos, they're a shoo-in for navy SEALs training or a trip to the funny farm."

He smiled his appreciation of the joke. A day with her family showed him where she derived her great sense of humor.

"My experience with family gatherings is pretty limited."

"Well, you're a hit. You officially passed inspection by the Carano brothers."

"Carano brothers." He held up his Groucho glasses. "Sounds like a family of mobsters."

"Shh. Don't say that too loud. We are Italian, remember."

They grinned into each other's eyes. From inside the house came a shout of "Touchdown."

The Cowboys must have scored. Here in the yard, the sounds were quieter, the splash of kids sliding into the pool, the occasional yip of the dog.

Though he'd felt out of place all afternoon, Collin liked Mia and her family. A couple of times he'd seen Mrs. Carano, who insisted on being called Rosalie, pat Mitchell's back and ply him with goodies from the family bakery. The kid must be ready to explode, but he'd soaked up the attention like Happy did, as though starved for positive reinforcement.

Had he been like that? He couldn't recall. He'd spent so much time keeping Drew out of trouble and Ian fed and safe that he really didn't remember ever being a child.

Mia swirled the melting ice round and round in her own glass, then pressed the coldness to the side of her neck. Collin's belly reacted to the feminine sight. Mia, with her nice family, her chatterbox ways and her honest concern for people was putting holes in his arguments against social workers. Except for the title and the business suits, she didn't fit the stereotype. Adam hadn't helped any with his innuendoes.

"You won Gabe over when your phone played 'Boomer Sooner.'" A soft smile lifted her pretty mouth, setting a single tiny dimple into relief. He'd never noticed that dimple before.

"I saw the Oklahoma Sooner tag on a couple of cars out there." He didn't bother to say Adam had grilled him about his intentions. No point in embarrassing Mia about a simple misunderstanding. Adam was a good guy. He'd meant well. Even if he was badly misguided.

"We all attended OU. Adam played a little baseball, so we're pretty hard-core Sooner fans. Gabe even has season tickets to the football games."

Collin had never made it to college. "I'm a big football fan myself." Which had made conversation with the Caranos a little easier.

"But not of the Dallas Cowboys. Nic is a little miffed about that, though he thinks he can convert you."

"Want me to lie to him since it's his birthday?"

She punched his arm. "Silly."

"Bully." He rubbed the spot just over his shamrock. A lot of people had asked him about the tattoo before and he'd told them nothing. But Mia was different. She had a way of slipping under his guard, catching him unawares, and the next thing he knew he was telling her way too much.

"I never liked tattoos before. But I like yours," she said as if reading his mind. "When did you have it done?"

"When I was seventeen." He wasn't about to tell her the shape he'd been in when he'd gone to the tattoo parlor.

"Isn't it illegal to get one at that age?"

"I wasn't a cop then."

He'd made the remark to encourage a smile. She didn't disappoint him.

"Well, even if it was illegal, you were very insightful to choose a tattoo that represents so much."

"Yeah. Real insightful." To him the tattoo represented a man, a cop at that, who couldn't find the brothers he'd promised to look after. It represented years of failure. He made a wry face. "I chose a shamrock because I needed space for three words and I like the color green."

Undaunted by his dry tone, she studied the figure. "Three leaves, three brothers. Your names are Irish. And green means everlasting, like the evergreen trees. Everlasting devotion."

He blinked down at the tattoo. Then at her.

She came to his shoulders and he could see the top of her hair. In the bright sunlight, the soft waves gleamed more red than brown. He defeated the sudden and unusual urge to touch her hair.

The tattoo had come about on what would have been Ian's twelfth birthday. Collin had been fighting a terrible depression, and the tattoo seemed like a grown-up, proactive thing to do at the time. Now he looked back on the day with a sense of chagrin and failure.

That had been a tough time for him. His days of being cared for in the foster system had been coming to an end, and he was scared out of his mind. He had no place to go, no training, no family, no money. Only a dim memory of two brothers to cling to and the fish keychain that somehow bound the three of them together. Then as now, every time he smoothed his fingers over the darkening metal, he felt closer to Drew and Ian.

"I can't say I was all that deep and symbolic about a tattoo, Mia. I think I was just hoping for a little good luck." He'd needed all the help he could get in the days following his eighteenth birthday.

"Did it work?"

She tilted her head back against the white siding and stared out at the pool where Mitch splashed with Gabe's ten-year-old son. Abby, Gabe's wife, watched from a lawn chair.

"Nah. Mostly, I think we make our own luck. What about you? Got a rabbit's foot in your purse?"

She smiled, but her eyes remained serious.

"I don't put much stock in luck, either. God, on the other hand, is a different matter. I truly believe He, not luck or coincidence, controls my destiny."

"Like a robot?"

She laughed and shook her head. The reddish waves danced back from her pretty face. "Not like that. People have free will. But if we let Him, God will guide our lives and work everything out for our good."

"You really think that?"

"Yes. I really do."

Well, he didn't. He thought you had to claw and fight and struggle uphill, hoping like mad that some crumb of good would fall in your lap.

"I always figured God was out there somewhere, but He was probably too busy to bother with one person."

"God's not like that, Collin. He's very personal. He cares about the smallest, simplest things in our lives."

"If that's so, why is there so much trouble in the world? Why do kids go hungry and parents mistreat and abandon them?" And why couldn't he find his brothers?

The seed of bitterness he tried to hide rose up like a sickness in his throat.

Mia placed a hand on his arm, a gentle, reassuring touch much like the ones he'd seen Rosalie give to Mitchell. He wanted her to stop. "I hear what you're not saying."

Of course she would. She dealt with people in his shoes all the time. She was trained to read behind the mask, a scary prospect if ever there was one. He didn't want anybody messing around inside his mind.

While his insides churned and he wondered what he was doing here, Collin tossed the remaining ice cubes onto a small bush growing beside the house. When the movement dislodged Mia's hand from his arm, he suffered a pang of loss. Talk about messed up. One minute he wanted her to stop touching him, and the next he was disappointed because she did.

"God can help you find your brothers," she said. "Or at least find out what happened to them."

He kept quiet. Mia had a right to her faith even if he had never witnessed anything much from God.

He rolled the empty glass back and forth between his palms. "Like I said, I don't know much about religion."

"That's okay. Faith's not about religion anyway."

She was losing him again.

"Faith is about having a relationship with the most perfect friend you could ever have. Jesus is a friend who promises to stick closer than a brother."

"Closer than a brother," he murmured softly. And then for some reason, he slid a hand into his pocket, found the tiny fish. The metal was warm from his body heat. "For me that wouldn't be too close."

"Then why can't you stop looking for them? And why is your arm tattooed with their names?"

She had a point there. "I guess I'm trying to keep them close even though they're lost." He pulled the tiny ichthus from his pocket. "See this?"

Her expressive face couldn't hide her surprise. "A Jesus fish?"

"I suppose you want to know why I carry it if I'm not a believer?"

"Yes."

He started to tease and say he carried the fish for luck. But that wasn't true. His feelings were deeper than that though he wasn't sure he had the words to express them.

"The day my brothers and I were separated the school counselor gave us each one of these." He turned the fish over. The bright sunlight caught the faded engraving, *Jesus will never leave you nor forsake you.* He'd thought of that scripture often and hoped it was true. He hoped there was somebody in this world looking after Ian and Drew.

"I wonder if they still have theirs," she murmured quietly.

"Why would they keep a cheap little keychain?" But he hoped they had.

"You kept yours."

He rubbed a finger over the darkened engraving as he'd done dozens of times. This was his link, his connection to Drew and Ian. That link, religion aside, gave him comfort. And if he'd tried to pray a few times as a boy, asking the distant God for help, well, he'd been a kid who just didn't understand the facts of life.

He wished that God could do something about his lost brothers, but he didn't know how to believe in anything but himself. His own strength and determination had gotten him where he was today. He knew better than to rely on anyone or anything else.

Before he could say more, Nic came sprinting around from the opposite side of the house, an orange plastic water pistol in one hand.

Gabe was right behind him, squirting his own water pistol like mad.

"You're gonna pay, birthday boy," he roared. And from the looks of Gabe's soaked shirtfront, Nic had started the trouble.

With a wild hyena laugh, Nic turned and fired, squirting Gabe as well as the two innocent bystanders. Mia jumped aside with a squeal of laughter.

Oddly disappointed to have his strange conversation with Mia interrupted, Collin brushed a water droplet from his arm.

"And you said your family was functional."

They both laughed as Adam came running past, wearing the Groucho glasses and carrying two squirt guns with another stuck in his shirt pocket.

"Defend yourself," he yelled and tossed a purple plastic pistol in their general direction.

With quick reflexes, Collin caught the squirt gun. As soon as the toy hit his hand, a sudden flashback hit Collin square in the heart.

Drew and Ian armed with water guns they'd gotten somewhere chased him around the trailer. He'd hidden under the house, behind the dangling insulation, and unloaded on them when they'd discovered his whereabouts.

They had all squirted and yelled and chased until the night grew too dark to see each other. As they often did, they'd spent that night without adults, but for once they'd gone to bed smiling.

"Collin?" Mia said, touching the hand that held the water pistol. "What's wrong?"

Even the good memories hurt. All those years he'd missed. All the good times he and his brothers had deserved to have. Though he recognized the irrationality of his emotions, he envied the Caranos. They had what he wanted and would never have. The missing years could not ever be recaptured.

"I gotta go." He handed her the squirt gun and abruptly strode to the pool. "Time to roll, Mitchell."

He felt Mia's gaze on his back.

Mitchell was instantly protesting. "I don't wanna leave yet."

"Sorry. I have to work tomorrow." He did have to work. On his house.

Water sluicing off his hair and shoulders, body language screaming in protest, Mitchell pulled himself slowly out of the pool. He grumbled, "It's not fair."

"Yeah, well, life isn't fair, kid. Get used to it."

Mitch stopped and tilted his head back to look into Collin's face. "Are you mad at me?"

Collin relented the slightest bit. The kid had behaved himself today. No use making Mitch pay for his lousy mood. He hooked an elbow around the boy's wet head.

"I'm not mad."

Trailed by an unusually quiet Mia, they went into the house to bid a civil goodbye to all the Carano clan. Mitchell dragged through the house like a man condemned, gathered his clothes and shoes for departure. Rosalie bustled into the kitchen and came back with two foil-wrapped plates.

"Leftovers. You two could use a little meat on your bones."

A funny lump formed inside Collin's chest. Was this what a mother did? Just like on television? Did normal mothers fret over the children and make huge family dinners and nag everyone to eat more?

"Take them, Collin," Mia murmured. "Make her happy." She'd protested their departure with all the usual niceties, but his mind was made up. He couldn't be here among this family any longer. It was killing him.

"I hope you'll come back soon, Collin," Rosalie was saying. "And bring this boy." She patted Mitchell's head. "You come anytime you want to, Mitchell. A friend of Mia's is our friend, too."

Finally, when he could bear no more of their kindness, he worked his way out to the sidewalk.

Mia stood in the doorway. She looked uncertain, worried. "Thank you for coming, Collin."

"Our pleasure, huh, Mitch?"

"Yeah." Mitch's bottom lip was dragging the ground. He looped a towel around his neck and sawed the rough terry cloth back and forth.

Collin didn't want to answer the questions in Mia's eyes, so he turned and started toward his truck. The door behind him didn't close for several more seconds.

He'd gotten himself into this mess with Mia. He'd known from the beginning that a social worker only brought trouble. Now he was knee-deep in this big-brother thing with Mitch and stuck with the constant reminders of everything he and his brothers had missed out on. He knew that sounded selfish and envious. Maybe he was.

Long ago, he'd made peace with who he was as well as who he wasn't. He'd made a decent life for himself and, except for his fruitless search for Drew and Ian, he was happy most of the time.

There was an old adage that said you don't miss what you've never had. He'd always thought it was a lie. Today confirmed his suspicion.

He wished he'd never come here.

Halfway down the sidewalk, Mitch asked, "Can I have Miss Carano bring me out to your house tomorrow afternoon?"

"Miss Carano goes to church. She's not your personal chauffeur."

"I can walk then. No big deal."

"Five miles?"

"I could borrow a bike."

When Collin didn't answer, Mitchell said, "I guess you don't want me to. That's cool. It's okay. I got plenty of stuff to do."

They walked in silence, Collin feeling like a major jerk. He didn't want the kid around right now. He wanted to be alone, to sort out whatever was eating a hole in him.

One hand on the truck door, Mitchell said, "Will you soak Happy's foot for me? I promised him, ya know."

That clinched it. The little dog *was* making progress with Mitch's tender, relentless care. "Be ready at one. I'll pick you up."

He was in over his head. He had agreed to mentor Mitchell indefinitely, and he wasn't a man to go back on his word. But Mia's brothers with their camaraderie and craziness stirred up a nest of hornets inside him. The reminders were there, too strong to ignore.

He'd have to set up some ground rules if he was to keep his sanity. Working with Mia was part of the deal but mentoring didn't have to include her family. If she wanted Mitch to experience family relationships she could bring him here herself. He was never coming back to this place again.

Mia sat on the floor of her office surrounded by bent, bedraggled cardboard boxes filled with old files dating back more than twenty years. Three weeks ago she'd hauled these files over from the storage room and had been going through them a few at a time whenever she could break away from her caseload.

So far, dust and an occasional spider were the only things she'd found. The task was, after all, a daunting one that could take years to turn up something. If it ever did.

With the back of her hand she scratched her nose, itchy from the stale smell and dust mites. The Lord had sent Collin Grace her way, and she wouldn't let a little thing like twenty years and a mountain of dusty files stop her from trying to show him that God cared enough to help him find his brothers.

"You busy?"

She looked up to find Adam standing in the doorway. He held out a tall paper cup. "Could you use a break?"

"I hope that's a cherry icy." She took the cup, peeked under the lid and said, "You are the best brother on the planet."

"Does that mean you'll help me clean my apartment this weekend?"

"I knew there was a catch." She sipped the cold drink, let the cool, clean sweetness wash away some of the dust. "New girlfriend coming over?"

He grinned sheepishly. "How did you know?"

Mia chuckled. Every time Adam started dating someone new he went into a cleaning frenzy. Only he wanted Mia to do the cleaning. And the redecorating. And the cooking.

"As long as I don't have to repaint this time."

"We only repainted last time because Mandy isn't a big sports fan."

And Adam's living room had been painted in red and white with a Red Sox insignia emblazoned on the ceiling. "I knew she wouldn't last long."

"If only I were as wise...." He toasted her with his fountain drink. "Which reminds me, I brought some information by for you to take to your new guy."

She eyed him from beneath a piece of floppy hair. "Excuse me? I haven't had a date in four months. There is no new guy."

"Collin. The cop." He made himself comfortable on the floor beside her. From inside his jacket he extracted an envelope, handing it to her.

"He's a friend, Adam." She read Collin's name on the front of the envelope. "Is this about that lawsuit?"

Adam nodded, but wouldn't be deterred from his original intent of matchmaking. "A few weeks ago you didn't even like the guy. The relationship is progressing pretty fast if you ask me."

"There is no relationship." Even if she wanted there to be, Collin had an invisible shield around him that held others at arm's length. "Ever since the birthday party he's been different. Cooler than usual." And for someone like Collin, that was as cool as this slush.

"He left soon after we started the water fight. Do you think we scared him off somehow?"

She'd wondered the same thing, though she couldn't imagine anything scaring a tough cop like Collin. "I don't know. Collin's hard to read sometimes. He holds a lot of himself in reserve."

From the bare-bones information Collin had shared about his childhood, he had every reason to distrust other human beings. But Mia didn't like the idea that he distrusted her, which accounted for her redoubled efforts to find some bit of information for him in these files. Trust had to be earned. And she wanted his.

"I keep wondering if we offended him somehow." He'd been fine while they were talking.

"Anyone who listens to Grandpa tell that story about the nanny goat and doesn't run at the first opportunity is not easily offended. Did he mention anything about why they left so early?"

She'd been out to his farm on a regular basis since the party, but their conversations had mostly been about Mitchell's latest truancy from school and the rescued animals. Once they'd talked about his search and another time he'd shocked her to no end by asking a question about God. She'd been frustrated to have no answer, but thrilled to know he was thinking about spiritual matters.

She rifled through another file, saw nothing related to Collin or his brothers and reached for another.

"Only that he appreciated our hospitality, thought we were a great family. You know, the usual polite stuff. And he thought the afternoon had been good for Mitchell."

Adam took the file folder from her hand and stuck it back in the box. "The boy needs a lot of attention. Did you see Mama plying him with cookies and questions?"

"Mama thinks food is the answer to everyone's problems."

"Isn't it?"

"My hips seem to think so." Every time Mia decided to do something about her few extra pounds, Mama invited her over for pasta and bread or asked her to work a few hours at the bakery. Or she went through a mini-crisis and baked some marvelous creation for herself. Having a family in the bakery business was both a blessing and a terrible temptation.

"So, do you like him?"

"Mitchell? Sure. He's basically a good boy, but he needs a firm hand and a strong role model. He went to Sunday School with me last week."

Adam gave her a look reserved for thick-headed sisters. "I'm talking about Collin."

"And I'm not." Every time a new man appeared on the horizon, her brothers zeroed in like stealth missiles.

"I can hope, can't I?"

"Not in this case." Though there was something about Collin that kept him on her mind all the time, she knew better than to let her feelings take over. She wanted God to choose the right man for her.

"Want me to beat him up? Get things moving?"

She laughed. "You know how I feel about the whole husband-hunting thing. God's timing is always perfect."

"If God is going to send you a husband, He needs to hurry."

"Adam," she admonished. But she had to admit to a certain restlessness lately. Though her job and her community and church activities kept her life more than busy, she had always planned to be married with a big house filled with kids by now. "You're a fine one to talk. When are you going to find Miss Right and settle down?"

He shrugged a pair of shoulders that had plenty of women interested. "I want what Mom and Dad have. I'm willing to wait as long as it takes to get it."

And she was willing to wait as well. She only hoped she didn't have to wait forever.

# *Chapter Eight*

An excited Mia jumped out of her Mustang, leaving her jacket behind and hurrying through the cool, windy evening to Collin's front door. In the west the sun was setting, a testament to the shorter days of late autumn.

The hollow sound of a hammer rang through the otherwise quiet countryside. Not once in the months since meeting him had she come to this house and found Collin idle. He was either working on the house, with the animals or helping Mitchell do something. Didn't the man ever lie around on the couch like a slob the way her brothers did?

She waited for a pause in the hammering and then pounded hard on the door. She'd finally found something and she couldn't wait to share the news with Collin.

"Collin, hello."

The hammering ceased. After a minute, she saw movement from the corner of her eye and heard Collin's voice. She spotted him near the side of the house, the area still mostly in skeleton form.

In the fading light, Collin raised the hammer in greeting, a smile lifting the corners of his mouth. Dressed in jeans and a denim shirt, he wore a tool belt slung low on his hips.

"Hey," he said.

She started toward him, her heart doing a weird ker-thumping action. Okay, so she was glad to see him. And yes, he was good-looking enough to make any woman's heart beat a little faster. But she was excited because of the news she had, not because Collin had smiled as if he was glad to see her, too. Mostly.

Adam and his insinuations were getting to her.

"Watch your step." Collin gestured at the pile of tools strewn about on the concrete pad, and then reached out to put a hand under her elbow.

His was a simple act of courtesy, but her silly heart did that ker-thump thing again. Come to think of it, this was the first time Collin had ever intentionally touched her.

A naked light bulb dangled from an extension cord in one corner to illuminate the work space. The smell and fog of sawdust hung cloud-like above a pile of pale new boards propped beside a table saw.

"I finally have the decking on top," he said with some satisfaction, unmindful of her sudden awareness of him as a man. "Even if the room won't be completely in the dry before the really cold weather sets in, I'll be able to work out here."

Usually Mitchell was under foot, pounding and sawing under Collin's close supervision. She looked around, saw no sign of the boy. "Where's Mitchell?"

Collin placed the hammer on a makeshift table, his welcoming expression going dark. "I caught him smoking in the barn. Took him home early."

"Oh, no. I thought you'd made him see the senselessness of cigarettes."

"Yeah, well that was a big failure, I guess." He sighed, a heavy sound, and ran both hands up the back of his head. "He's been acting up again. Mouthy. Moody. Maybe I'm not doing him any good after all."

"Don't think that, Collin. All kids mess up, regress. But he's come a long way in a short time. The school says he's only missed two days since you spoke to his class on careers in law enforcement. His discipline referrals for fighting are down, too."

He squinted at her. "You know what he's been fighting about?"

"No. Do you?"

"I've got a clue." He turned to the closed door leading into the living area. "Come on in. You're getting cold."

Pleasure bloomed. He'd noticed.

Inside the kitchen, he motioned toward a half-full Mr. Coffee. "Coffee?"

"Sure." She took the offered cup, wrapping her hands around the warmth. "Are you going to share your insights with me?"

Collin leaned a hip against the clean white counter. If she was a betting woman, she'd bet he'd laid the tile himself. "I think Mitch is under a lot of pressure from some of the other boys."

"What kind of pressure?"

"I haven't figured that part out. There's something though. I have a feeling it has to do with his stepdad. That's a very sore subject lately."

Her caseworker antennae went up. "Anything I need to investigate on a professional basis?"

Over the rim of his coffee cup, Collin gave her the strangest look, a look she'd come to recognize each time she mentioned her job. He took a long time in answering such a simple question.

"I guess it wouldn't hurt to keep your eyes and ears open."

She was already doing that.

"How's Happy?"

"Still happy." He grinned at his own joke and pulled a chair around from the table to straddle the seat. "Doc says the foot is still in danger. It'll kill Mitchell if she has to amputate."

She could tell Collin wouldn't be too happy either, but he wasn't about to say so.

"He's attached."

"Very." Arms folded over the back of the chair, the coffee mug dangled from his fingers.

"You are, too."

He made a face. "Yeah."

And she was glad to know he could form bonds this way, even though they saddened him. Some kids who grew up in the system were never able to love and bond.

"I have a bit of news for you." She laid her purse on the table and pulled out a slip of paper.

"I could use some today. Shoot."

"This may turn out to be nothing, but—" she handed him the note "—this is the address of foster parents who took care of one of your brothers shortly after you were separated. They're not on your list."

The expression on his face went from mildly interested to intense. "Seriously?"

"The address hasn't been updated and there was no telephone, so we may not find anything."

He shoved out of the chair and grabbed a jacket. "Let's go see."

"Collin, wait."

He paused, face impassive.

Suddenly, she regretted her impulsive action to come here first before checking out the address herself.

"I haven't made contact. We don't know if anything will come from this. Don't get your hopes up, okay?"

"It's worth a shot." He shrugged the rest of the way into his jacket. "We'll take my truck."

She had known he'd react this way, pretending not to hope, but grasping at anything. If the foster parents were still around, they might not remember one little boy who passed through their lives so long ago. And if they did, they probably wouldn't remember where the child had gone from there.

"This is the first new piece of the puzzle I've had in a long time," Collin admitted as he smoothly guided the truck around the orange barrels and flashing lights of the ever-present road construction that plagued Oklahoma City. "Dartmouth Drive is back in one of these additions. I've been out here on calls. Not the best part of town."

A bad feeling came over her. She felt the need to say one more time, "Remember, now. This address comes from a very old file."

"I heard you." But she could tell that he didn't want to think that the trip might be futile.

Night had fallen and the wind picked up even more. An enormous harvest moon rose in the east. Mia had a sense of trepidation about approaching a strange house at night.

"Maybe we should have waited until tomorrow."

"I've waited twenty years." The lights of his vehicle swept over a wind-wobbled sign proclaiming Dartmouth Drive. He turned onto a residential street. "Should be right down here on the left."

She could feel the tension emanating from him like heat from a stove. He wanted to find out something new about his brothers so badly. And now that they were nearing the place, Mia was scared. If the trip proved futile, would he be devastated?

"Here's the address." He pulled the truck to a stop along the curb.

She squinted into the darkness. "I don't think anyone is at home, Collin."

"Maybe they watch TV with the lights off."

They made their way up the cracked sidewalk. In the moonlight Mia observed that the grass was overgrown, a possibility only if no one had been here for a long time. Growing season had been over for more than a month.

She shouldn't have let him come here and be disappointed. But she'd been so excited that she hadn't thought everything through in advance. She'd only wanted to give him hope. Now, Collin could be hurt again because of her.

He banged on the front door.

"Collin," she said softly, wanting to touch him, to comfort him.

He ignored her and banged again, harder. "Hello. Anybody home?"

"Collin." This time she did touch him. His arm was like granite.

He stared at the empty, long-abandoned house. In the moonlight, his jaw worked. She heard him swallow and knew he swallowed a load of disappointment.

Abruptly, he did an about-face. "Dry run."

Inside the truck, Mia said, "This was my fault. I'm so sorry."

He gripped the steering wheel and stared at the empty house. "I should be used to it by now."

That small admission, that no matter how many times he came up empty he still hurt, broke Mia's heart. She couldn't imagine the pain and loneliness he'd suffered in his life. She couldn't imagine the pain of being separated from her loved ones the way Collin had been.

When they'd first met, she'd thought him cold and heartless. Now she realized what a foolish judgment she'd made.

Because she didn't know what else to do, Mia closed her eyes and prayed. Prayed for God to help them find Drew and Ian. Prayed that Collin could someday release all his heartache to the only One who could heal him. Prayed that she would somehow find the words to compensate for her bad judgment.

In silence they drove out of the residential area and headed toward Collin's place and her vehicle. Mia was glad she'd left her car at the farm. Collin didn't need to be alone even if he thought he did.

"Are you okay?" she finally asked.

In the dim dash lights he glanced her way, his cop face expressionless. "Sure. You hungry?"

The question had her turning in her seat. "Hungry?"

"As in food. I haven't had dinner."

"Neither have I." She felt out of balance. He had

shoved aside what had to be, at least, a disappointment. Was this the way he handled his emotions? By ignoring them?

They parked behind a popular steak house and went inside.

They passed a buffet loaded with steaming vegetables and a variety of meats that had her mouth watering.

"You look confused," Collin said as he held a chair for her.

She was. In more ways than one. "I was expecting a tofu bar with bean sprouts and seaweed."

"I eat what I like."

There went another assumption she shouldn't have made about him.

They filled their plates from the hot bar and found a table. Collin had ordered a steak as well.

"Comfort food?" she asked gently after the waitress brought their drinks and departed.

He shrugged. "Just hungry. This place makes great steaks."

She squeezed the lemon slice into her tea.

"Want mine?" Collin said, removing the slice from the edge of his glass.

"You're giving up vitamin C?" She teased, but took the offered fruit. "Do you eat out like this all the time?"

"Not that much. Mostly I cook for myself."

She should have figured as much. He'd been self-reliant of necessity all of his life, a notion that made her heart hurt. But that strength had made him good at about anything he set his mind to. She wondered if he knew that about himself and decided that he didn't.

"What's your specialty?" she asked.

"Meat loaf and mashed potatoes. How about you? You live alone, too. Do you eat at your folks' or cook for yourself?"

"For myself most of the time. Although I sneak over to the bakery a little more often than I should."

"You any good?"

"Look at this body." With a self-deprecating twist of her mouth, she held her hands out to the side. "What do you think?"

"I think you look great." His brown eyes sparkled with appreciation.

"That wasn't what I meant." A rush of heat flooded her neck. "I meant—"

He laughed and let her off the hook. "I know what you meant." He pointed a fork at her. "But you still look good."

"Well." She wasn't sure what to say. She got her share of compliments, but she'd never expected one from Collin. He was full of surprises tonight. "Thank you."

The waitress brought his steak and they settled in to eat, making comments now and then about the food. After a bit the conversation lagged and all she could think about was the night's failed trip. Collin might want to ignore the subject, but Mia would explode if she didn't get her feelings out in the open.

"Will you let me apologize for not checking out that address before telling you about it?"

"No use talking the subject to death."

"We haven't talked about it at all." Which was driving her nuts.

"Just as well." He laid aside his fork and took a man-size drink of tea.

"Not really. Talking helps you sort out your feelings, weigh your options." And made her feel a whole lot better.

Collin looked at her, steady and silent. If anyone was going to talk, she would have to be the one.

"I'll keep looking. The information has to be there somewhere. We'll find them."

"You could check the adoption files. See if either of my brothers was adopted."

"I'm checking those."

Attention riveted to his plate, he casually asked, "The sealed ones?"

Her breath froze in her throat. "I won't do that."

He looked up. The naked emotion in his eyes stunned her. "Why not?"

Shoulders instantly tense, she had to remind him, "I told you from the beginning I wouldn't go into sealed files."

"That was before you knew me. Before we were friends."

Friends? "Is that what the compliment was about? To soften me up?"

His jaw tightened. "Is that what you think?"

She leaned back in her chair, miserable to be at odds with him over this. "No. Not really, but I can't believe you'd ask me to do such a thing."

Anger flared in the normally composed face. His fork clattered against his plate. "Wanting to find my brothers is not a crime. I'm not some do-wrong trying to ferret out information for evil purposes. This is my life we're talking about."

"I know that, Collin. But the files are closed for a reason. Parents requested and were given sealed records because they wanted the promise of privacy. And until those people request a change, those files have to stay sealed."

He crammed a frustrated hand over his head, spiking the hair up in front. "Nearly twenty-five years of my life is down the drain, Mia. I need to find them. They're men now. Opening those files won't hurt them or anybody else."

She shook her head, sick at heart. "I can't. It's wrong. Please understand."

Back rigid, he pushed away from the table and stood. The cold mask she'd encountered the first time they'd met was back in place.

# *Chapter Nine*

Collin was not having a good day. In fact, the last two had been lousy.

He pushed the barn door open, stopping in the entrance to breathe in the warm scents of animals, feed and the ever-present smell of disinfectant. He went through gallons of the stuff trying to protect the sick animals from each other.

Since the night he'd let himself hope, only to be slapped down again, he'd battled a growing sense of emptiness.

After work tonight he'd gone to the gym with Maurice and true to form, his buddy had invited him home for dinner and Bible study. For the first time, he'd wanted to go. But he always felt so out of place in a crowd. And a Bible study was a whole different universe.

Not that he hadn't given God a lot of thought lately. Every time he showered or changed shirts and noticed his shamrock, Mia's words rang in his memory. She had something in her life that he didn't. And that something was more than a big, noisy family. Maurice had the same thing, so Collin figured the difference must be God.

One of the horses nickered as Collin moved down the dirt-packed corridor. These animals depended on him, regardless of the kind of day he'd had. He could take care of himself. They couldn't.

As was his habit, he headed to Happy's pen first. The little dog's attitude could lighten him up no matter what.

Mitchell, whom he hadn't seen since the smoking incident, was already inside the stall.

Irritation flared. The little twerp had some nerve coming back around the animals without permission.

Collin was all prepared to give him a tongue-lashing and send him home when the boy looked up.

What he saw punched him in the gut.

The kid's face was bruised from the eyebrow to below the cheekbone. A sliver of bloodshot eye showed through the swelling.

"What happened?" He heard his own voice, hard and angry.

Mitchell dropped his head, fidgeting with the dog brush in his hands. "I won't smoke anymore, Collin."

"Not what I asked."

Mitchell jerked one narrow shoulder. "Nothing."

With effort, Collin forced a calm he didn't feel. "Home or school?"

The boy was silent for a minute. Then he blew out a gust of air as if he'd been holding his breath, afraid Collin would send him away. "Not my mom."

The stepdad then. Collin had run a check on Teddy Shipley. He had a rap sheet longer than the road from here to California, where he'd spent a year in the pen for assault with a deadly weapon and manufacturing an illegal substance. A real honey of a guy.

Collin hunkered down beside the boy, rested one hand lightly on the skinny back. "You can tell me anything."

Mitchell developed a sudden fascination with the bristles of Happy's brush. He flicked them back and forth against his palm. "I can't."

And then he dropped the brush and buried his face in Happy's thick fur. Happy, true to his name, moaned in ecstatic joy and licked at the air.

The kid was either scared or he knew something that would incriminate someone he cared about. And the cop in Collin suspected who.

He sighed wearily. Life could be so stinking ugly. "If he hits you again, I'm all over him."

Mitch's head jerked up. His one good eye widened. "I never told you that. Don't be saying I did."

Compassion, mixed with frustration, pushed at

the back of Collin's throat. He clamped down on his back teeth, hating the feelings.

"Did you go to school like this?"

Mitch shook his head. "No."

So that's why he'd shown up here this evening. Things were out of hand at home.

"Does he hit your mom, too?"

Tears welled in the boy's eyes. "She'd be real mad if she knew I told."

"Why?"

"She just would."

What Mitch wasn't saying spoke volumes. Collin had seen this scenario before. He'd also lived it.

Violence. Codependence. Drugs. A mother who preferred the drugs and a violent man to the safety and well-being of herself and her child. He wouldn't be a bit surprised if Teddy was cooking meth again, a suspicion that deserved checking into.

The sound of a car engine had Mitchell scrubbing frantically at his face. Collin turned toward the interruption. He'd know that Mustang purr anywhere. Mia. Just who he did not want to see. A social worker who'd stick her nose into something she couldn't fix. He was a cop. He could handle the situation far better than she could.

Mitch leaped up, recognizing the car as well. His one good eye widened in panic. "Don't say anything, huh, Collin?"

Like she wouldn't notice an eye swollen shut.

"Go brush down the colt and give him a block of hay," he said, giving the kid an out. If Mia didn't see him, she wouldn't ask questions, and no one would have to lie.

Mitch shot out of the pen, disappearing into the far stall.

Collin picked up an empty feed sack and crushed it into a ball.

His world had been orderly and uneventful until Mia had come barging into it, hounding him, talking until he'd said yes to shut her up. And then her family had gotten in on the deal. First the birthday party. Then Adam's help with the lawsuit. And now Leo, Mia's father, found daily reasons why Collin had to stop by the bakery. Try as he might, Collin couldn't seem to say no.

Man. What had he gotten himself into?

The colt whickered. One of the dogs started barking. And the whole menagerie began moving restlessly.

Collin didn't rush out to greet his visitor. He needed some time to think. Still baffled by Mia's stubbornness over something as simple as looking into a file, he wasn't sure what to say to her.

They didn't share the same sense of justice. He believed in obeying the law, but there was a difference in the spirit of the law and the letter of the law. To him, opening his own brothers' adoption files, if they existed, would fall under the spirit of the law. It was the right and just thing to do.

But he had to be fair to Mia, too. She'd gone above and beyond the call of duty in searching those moldy old files in the first place. And even if she was a pain in the backside sometimes, having her around lightened him somehow, as if the goodness in her could rub off.

After a minute's struggle, Collin decided to wait her out. Mia knew where he was if she had something to say. He'd known from the start he didn't want the grief of some woman trying to get inside his head. He had enough trouble inside there himself.

He went to work scrubbing down a newly emptied pen. The last stray, hit by a car, hadn't made it. He'd been hungry too long to have the strength to fight.

Fifteen minutes later, when Mia hadn't come storming inside the barn, smiling and rattling off at the mouth, Collin began to wonder if he'd heard her car at all. He dumped the last of the bleach water over the metal security cage and went to find out.

Sure enough, Mia's yellow Mustang sat in his driveway but she was nowhere to be seen.

Mitch came to stand beside him, one of Panda's adolescent kittens against his chest. "Where is she?"

"Beats me."

At that very moment, she flounced around the side of the house, her sweater flapping open in the stiff wind. She wasn't wearing her usual smile. Almond eyes shooting sparks, she marched right up to Collin.

"I don't stop being a friend because of a disagreement."

That didn't surprise him. The sudden lift in his mood did. Renewed energy shot through his tired muscles. He hid a smile. Mia was pretty cute when she got all wound up.

She slapped a wooden spoon against his chest.

"I brought food. Home-cooked." She tilted her head in a smug look. "And you are going to love it."

He fought the temptation to laugh. Normally, when a woman pushed too hard, she was history, but with Mia he couldn't stay upset. That fact troubled him, but there it was.

Unmindful of the sparks flying between the adults, Mitch stepped between them. "Food. Cool."

Mia started to say something then stopped. Her mouth dropped open. She stared at Mitchell's bruised face, expression horrified. "What happened to you?"

Mitchell shot Collin a silent plea and then hung his head, averting his battered face.

"I got in a fight."

"Oh, Mitch." And then her fingers gently grazed the boy's cheekbone in a motherly gesture. The tension in Mitch's shoulders visibly relaxed, but his eyes never met Mia's.

Collin let the lie pass for now. Whether Mitch liked the idea or not, a cop was mandated by law to share his suspicions with the proper authorities, and that was Mia. If there was any possibility that a child was in danger, welfare had a right to know. The policeman in him accepted that regardless of his personal aversion.

"I'm starved," he said, knowing his statement would be an effective diversion. Mia's respondent smile washed through him warm and sweet, like a spring wind through a field of flowers. "Cleaning pens can wait until after dinner."

"Not mad at me anymore?" she asked.

Quirking one brow, he started toward the house and left her to figure that out for herself. He wasn't sure he knew the answer anyway.

The early sunsets of November were upon them and the wind blew from the north promising a change in weather. Leaves loosened their tree-grip and tumbled like tiny, colorful gymnasts across the neatly fenced lots housing the grazers. The deer with the bad hip had healed and now roamed restlessly up and down the fence line longing to run free. Collin and Doc had decided to wait until after hunting season ended to give the young buck a fighting chance.

When they reached the house, Collin opened the door and let Mia and Mitchell enter first. The smell of Italian seasoning rushed out and swirled around his nose.

"Smells great. What is it?" Not that he cared—a home-cooked Italian dinner was too good to pass up. Especially one cooked by Mia.

"Lasagna. Wash your hands. Both of you." She shooed them toward the sink. "Food's still hot."

Along with Mitchell, he meekly did as he was told, scrubbing at the kitchen sink. If anyone else came into his house issuing orders and rummaging in his cabinets, he would be furious. Weird that he wasn't bothered much at all.

While Mia rattled forks and thumped plates onto his tiny table, he murmured to Mitch, "A lie will always come back to bite you. Better tell her."

Mitchell darted a quick glance at Mia and gave his head a slight shake, his too-long hair flopping forward to hide his expression. Collin let the subject drop. For now.

Moments later, they dug into the meal. Collin could barely contain a moan of pleasure.

Lifting a forkful of steaming noodles and melted mozzarella, he said, "If this is your idea of a peace offering, I'll get mad at you more often."

Mia sliced a loaf of bread and pushed the platter toward him. Steam curled upward, bringing the scent of garlic and yeast.

"There are still things I can do to help, Collin. Unlike foster-care files, many of the adoption files have been computerized. I started searching the open ones today."

He took a chunk of the bread and slathered on a pat of real butter. "Are the sealed files on computer, too?"

There was a beat of silence, and then, "It doesn't matter."

She wasn't budging from her hard-nosed stand.

"After all the years I've searched and come up

empty, I think the adoption files are the answer. They have to be."

Mitchell was already digging in for seconds. "Why are you trying to get into adoption files?"

Collin started. He never spoke openly about his brothers or his past. He'd never before said a word about them in front of Mitchell. Was this what hanging around with a chatterbox did for a guy? He started to lie to the boy, and then remembered his words only moments before. A lie would always come back to haunt you.

"I'm looking for my brothers," he said honestly. "We were separated in foster care as kids."

Saying the words aloud didn't seem so hard this time.

"No kidding?" Mitch backhanded a string of cheese from his mouth. "You were a foster kid?"

"Yeah. I was." He held his breath. Would the knowledge lessen him in Mitchell's eyes?

Mitch's one unblemished eye, brown and serious, studied him in awe. "But you became a cop. How'd you do that?"

And just that simply, Collin experienced a frisson of pride instead of shame. Mia had been right all along. Mitch needed to know that the two of them shared some commonalities.

"A lousy childhood doesn't have to hold you back."

By now, the boy's mouth was jammed full again, so he just nodded and chewed. He chased the food with a gulp of iced tea and then said, "So where are your brothers? Can Miss Carano find them? Can't the police find them? I'll help you look for them. How many do you have?"

His words tumbled out, eager and naive.

Collin filled him in on the bare facts. "And Miss Carano's helping me search, too. Even though I've been a pain about it."

He gave her his version of an apologetic look. He wasn't sorry for asking her to bend the rules a little, but he was glad to be back on comfortable footing with her. The last couple of days had been lousy without her.

"I've started a hand search of the old records in the storage room of the municipal building," Mia told him. "That's where I found that address the other day."

The police records were warehoused the same way, and he knew from experience that hand searches were tedious and time-consuming. And often fruitless.

"I appreciate all you're doing, Mia. Honestly. But you can't blame me for wanting to investigate every available option."

"I don't blame you." She pushed her plate aside and said, "Anyone for dessert?"

"Dessert?" Both males moaned at the same time.

"You should have warned us." Collin put a hand over his full belly. He looked around the tiny kitchen, spotted a covered container on the bar. "What is it?"

Mia laughed. "My own made-from-scratch cherry chocolate bundt cake. But we can save dessert for later."

"You made it yourself?"

"Yep. The bread and lasagna, too."

The sweet Italian bread *must* have come from her parents' bakery. "No way."

"Way. I didn't grow up a baker's daughter for nothing. All of us kids cut our teeth on the old butcher-block table in the back of the bakery where Mom and Dad hand-mixed the dough for all kinds of cakes and breads and cookies."

She got up and started clearing the table. Collin grabbed the glasses.

"Let me help with this."

"I can get the dishes. Didn't you say you still have work in the barn?"

"Work can wait."

Mitchell, who looked as if he'd rather be anywhere but in a kitchen with unwashed dishes, piped up. "I'll do the rest of the chores outside. I don't mind."

With a knowing chuckle, Collin gave him instructions and let him go.

"Did you see the look on his face?"

"And to think he prefers mucking out stalls to our esteemed company." Mia feigned hurt.

In the tiny kitchen area, they bumped elbows at the sink. Collin didn't usually enjoy company that much, but over the weeks and months he'd known Mia, she'd become a part of his life. Sometimes an annoying part, but if he was honest, even when they disagreed he depended upon her to see through his anger to the frustration and still be his friend.

He'd never expected to call a social worker "friend."

At times, he could be brooding and moody, and admittedly, he wore a protective armor around his heart. Trouble was, Miss Mia had slipped beneath it at some point and discovered the softer side of him. The idea unhinged him.

"Thanksgiving's coming soon," she said, her voice coming from above a sink of soapy hot water. "We always have a big to-do at Mama's. Turkey, dressing, pecan pie. The works. The Macy's Thanksgiving Day parade on TV and then a veritable marathon of football games afterward."

He knew what was coming and didn't know what to do. Nic's birthday party had stirred up something inside him, a hunger for the things missing in his own life, and he wasn't sure he could go there again.

Mia rinsed a plate under the hot tap. As he reached to take the dish, she held on, forcing him to look down at her.

Green eyes, honey-sweet and honest, held his. "We'd love for you to come. Please say you will."

Steam rose up between them, moist and warm. Her eyes, her tone indicated more than an invitation of kindness to a man who had nowhere else to go. She really wanted him there.

Like most holidays, Thanksgiving was a family occasion. The time or two he'd accepted an invitation, he'd felt like an intruder. "I usually volunteer to work so the officers with families can be off that day."

"Then I'd say you're due a day off this year. Wouldn't you?"

"I'd better not."

Disappointment flashed across her face. Unlike him, she could never hide her feelings. They were there for the whole world to see. And what he saw both troubled and pleased him. Mia liked him. As more than a friend.

She let go of the plate and went back to washing. The air in the kitchen hung heavy with his refusal and her reaction. He didn't want to hurt her. In fact, he couldn't believe she was disappointed. Couldn't believe she'd be interested in him. He didn't belong with her all-American perfect family.

Mia, true to form, rushed in to the fill the quiet, and if he hadn't known better, her chatter would have convinced him that she didn't really care one way or the other. But now he knew her chatter sometimes covered her unease.

Then she mentioned some guy she'd met during the 10-K charity walk last weekend, and his mood turned from thoughtful to sour. If she was attracted to him, why was she having Starbucks with some runner?

He interrupted. "Wonder what's keeping Mitchell?"

Mia stopped in mid-sentence and gave him a funny look. "He hasn't been gone that long."

"Long enough." He tossed his dish towel over the

back of a chair that served as a towel rack, coat rack, whatever.

The water gurgled out of the sink. Mia dried her hands. "If you'll stop scowling, I'll go check. I need to get something out of my car anyway."

"I can go. He's my responsibility."

"Mine, too. You stay here and slice the cake. I have a book in the car for you."

"A Bible?" he asked suspiciously.

Tossing on her sweater, she laughed and opened the door. "You'll see."

Halfway out, she stopped and looked over her shoulder. "I want coffee with my cake."

The door banged shut and Collin found himself grinning into the empty space. Tonight Mia had made this half-finished, scantily furnished, poor excuse for a house feel like a home.

He turned that thought over in his head and went to make the lady's coffee.

Four scoops into the pot, a scream shattered the quiet. Coffee grounds went everywhere. His heart stopped.

"Mia."

He was out the door, running toward the barn before he realized the previously dark sky was lit with bright light. Fire light.

"Mitchell!"

He heard Mia's cry once more and this time he spotted her, running toward the burning barn. Before he could yell for her to stop, to turn back, she disappeared inside.

Collin thought he would die on the spot. Adrenaline ripped through his veins with enough force to knock him down. He broke into a run, pounding over the hard, dry ground.

Flames licked the sky. Sparks shot fifty feet up, fueled by the still wind. The horses screamed in terror. Dogs barked and howled. Several had managed to escape somehow and now scrambled toward him. A kitten streaked past, her fur smoking.

A horrible sense of doom slammed into him, overwhelming. Mia and Mitchell were inside a burning barn along with more than a dozen helpless, trapped, sick and injured animals.

He darted toward the outside water faucet, thankful for the burlap feed sack wrapped around the pipes to prevent freezing. Yanking the sack free, he dipped the rough cloth into the freshly filled trough then rushed into the barn just as Mitchell came stumbling out.

Collin caught him by the shoulders. "Where's Mia?"

Mitchell shook his head, coughing. "I don't know."

With no time to waste, he shoved Mitchell out into the fresh air. "Call 911."

He could only hope the boy obeyed.

And then he charged into the burning building.

Smoke, thick and blinding, wrapped him in a terrifying embrace.

"Mia!" he yelled as he slung the wet sack around his face and head.

Eyes streaming, lungs screaming, he traversed the interior by instinct, throwing open stalls and pens as he called out, over and over again. The animals would at least have a chance this way. Locked in, they would surely die.

He stumbled over something soft and pitched forward, slamming his elbow painfully into a wall. A familiar whine greeted him. When he reached down, the dog licked his hand. Happy.

With more joy than he had time to feel, he scooped the little dog up and headed him in the direction of the open doorway. Even a crippled dog would instinctively move toward the fresh air.

A timber above his head cracked. Honed reflexes moved him to one side as the flaming board thundered to the barn floor. If he stayed too long, he'd never make it out.

Another board fell behind him and then another. Common sense said for him to escape now. His heart wouldn't let him.

"Mia." His voice, hoarse and raspy, made barely a sound against the roaring, crackling fire. Heat seared the back of his hands. His head swam.

If something happened to her. If something happened to Mia.

Suddenly, he heard her coughing. And praying.

Renewed energy propelled him forward.

"I'm coming."

*Keep praying, Mia, so I can find you.*

With his free hand, he felt along the corridor wall. No longer could he hear animal sounds, but Mia's prayers grew louder.

In the dense darkness he never saw her, but he heard her and reached out, made contact. She frantically clawed at his arm.

"I've got you."

"Thank God. Thank God." A fit of harsh coughing wracked her. "Mitch," she managed.

"He's safe."

Without a thought, Collin stripped the covering from his face and pressed the rough fabric against Mia's mouth and nose. Her breath puffed hot and dry against his fingers.

"This way."

With his knowledge of the barn, he guided them away from the falling center toward the feed room. There, a small window would provide escape.

Though the seconds seemed to drag, Collin knew by the size of the fire that they'd been inside only a few minutes. Thankfully, the flames had not reached this section of the barn yet, but they were fast approaching.

"Hurry," he said needlessly, pushing and pulling her stumbling form.

Inside the feed room, he felt for the window, shoved the sash upward, then easily lifted Mia over the threshold and to safety on the ground.

A roar erupted behind him. The flames, as if enraged by Mia's escape, chased him. Licking along the wall, they found the empty paper sacks and swooshed into the room.

Collin scrambled up and out the window, falling to the ground below. What little air he had left was knocked out in the fall.

Mia grabbed his hand and tugged. "Get up. We have to get away."

Hands clasped, they stumbled around the side of the barn to an area several yards out from the flames. Mia fell to her knees, noisily sucking in the fresh air.

Collin went down beside her, filling his lungs with the sweet, precious oxygen.

"You okay?" he asked when he could breathe again.

"Fine."

But he couldn't take her word for it. By the flickering light of the fire that had nearly stolen her, he searched her face for signs of injury and found none.

"If anything had happened to you—"

And then before his reasonable side could stop him, he pulled her into his arms and kissed her.

She tasted smoky and sweet and wonderful. Emotion as foreign as an elephant and every bit as powerful coursed through him. His world tilted, spun, shimmered with warning.

He pulled back, suddenly afraid of what was happening to him. It was only a kiss, wasn't it? Given out of fear and relief. That was all. Only a kiss.

But he knew better. He'd kissed other women before, but not like this. The others he'd kept at a distance, outside of the armor. Mia was different. Way different.

And the truth of that scared him more than the barn fire.

# *Chapter Ten*

"Here Mitch, take this end down to Adam."

Mia stood in the yard of her parents' home surrounded by large plastic containers filled with Christmas lights and decorations. Twined around her shoulders and across her arms was a tangled strand of frosty icicle lights. Adam worked at the opposite end of the fence attaching the strands as she unraveled them.

The other Caranos were scattered about in the yard and over the exterior of the house in similar activity. Each year on a given Saturday, Rosalie commandeered all available family members to set up outside Christmas decorations while the weather was decent. Today was the day.

Mitch, eager for a promised turkey hunt with Mia's dad, was trying to hurry the process.

"Why are you putting up Christmas lights so early? We haven't even had Thanksgiving yet."

He took the proffered end of the lights and trudged toward Adam.

Mia squinted at him, the November sun bright, the wind light but sharp. "That's the whole point. At the Caranos, turning the lights on for the first time on Thanksgiving night is a big deal. You *are* still coming, aren't you?"

One narrow shoulder jerked. "I guess. Nothing else to do."

Mia recognized Mitch's unique method of saving face. Holidays at his house, from what he'd told her and from what she'd seen, were not festive occasions. And from the latest information Collin had shared, Mia was more concerned than ever. Life at the Perez house grew more troubled with each passing week, and Mitchell spent most of his time on the streets, or with her or her mother and dad to avoid going home. His was a worrisome situation indeed, especially with the added tension between Collin and Mitch since the fire.

"Sure he's coming," Adam hollered. "We're going to finish that computer chess tournament, and I'm going to beat the socks off him."

Mitch handed him the light cord and grinned. "Wanna bet?"

"If I win, you have to wash my car inside and out."

"When *I* win, I get to wear your OU jersey to school."

"No betting around here, boys," Rosalie called

from her spot on the front porch. She was winding greenery around the columns.

"Yes, ma'am," Adam replied, his swarthy face wreathed in ornery laughter. He loved to get Mama riled up.

"Yes, ma'am," Mitchell echoed, grinning at Adam.

Mia's dad came around the corner of the house, carrying the last of the nativity pieces that would grace their front yard. "As soon as I put this with the others, I'm going out to Collin's place."

Mia looked up in surprise, her pulse doing the usual flip-flop at Collin's name. "What for?"

Leo, like the other Caranos, had worked overtime to draw Collin into the fold. Though they'd yet to get him back to a large family gathering, he'd started hanging out with regularity at the Carano Bakery—at Leo's insistent invitation.

"Cops and donuts. They're a natural," her dad had said, but she knew he liked the quiet cop.

So did she.

"We need a couple of bales of hay to make the stable scene look authentic," Leo said. "I figured Collin might have some extra."

"Dad," Mia said, stricken at the memory. "Collin won't have any hay."

"Sure he will..." He stopped and set the manger down with a thud. "What was I thinking? All his hay went up with the barn."

"Yeah." Mitch scuffed a toe against the brown grass.

After their escape, while the firefighters drenched the glowing remains of the animal refuge, Collin had asked Mitch if he'd been smoking in the barn again. The question had devastated the boy. He hadn't been to the farm in the days since.

"He doesn't want me out there anymore."

"That's not true. He's upset right now because of the lost animals, but he's not upset with you."

"I could hear the puppies crying."

A heaviness tugged at Mia. They'd discussed this before, but the dying animals haunted him. "I know."

"I tried to find them, but the smoke was so bad."

She slid the lights from her shoulder and signaled Adam with a glance. He touched a finger to his eyebrow in silent agreement, understanding her need to counsel with Mitch. "Let's go sit on the porch and talk."

He followed her, slumping onto the step of the long concrete porch. Rosalie had moved down to the end post to add a red bow to the greenery.

"The investigators are still checking into the fire, but if you say you weren't smoking, I believe you."

"But Collin doesn't."

"I think he does, Mitchell, and he's sorry he hurt your feelings. He just has a hard time saying so."

"He's mad because of the puppies."

"No. He's sad. The same way you and I are."

The young boy stared morosely across the street where two squirrels gathered nuts beneath a pecan tree. "Do you think God cares about animals? Strays, I mean?"

She'd wondered when he'd ask something like that. Her faith was an open topic with anyone who knew her and the two of them had had more than one deep discussion.

"Sparrows aren't worth much in our eyes, but the Bible says God feeds them and watches over them." She pointed toward the squirrels. "And just look at those guys. God provided all the nuts they could ever want in that one tree. And they don't even have to buy them!"

Her attempt at humor fell flat. Mitchell wasn't in a joking mood.

"I'm going to miss them. Rascal and Slick and Milly and her kittens." Mitchell had named them all, something that had bothered Collin at first.

He gathered a handful of dead grass and tossed the blades one at a time.

"There would be something wrong with us if we didn't grieve over what we care about. But remember this one good thing—God allowed us to love them and give them a nice home in their last days. They hadn't had that before."

"Yeah. That's true." He tossed the remaining grass and wiped a hand down his jeans' leg. "I guess God is okay."

Mia draped an arm across Mitch's shoulders. "God is the best friend you could ever have, Mitchell."

"Is Collin a Christian?"

Something sharp pinched at her heart. "You'll have to ask him about that."

She wanted to believe that Collin would eventually accept Christ. Especially now. And not just because of Mitch's adoration, though that certainly loomed large. Mitch admired her Christian dad and brothers, too, but he shared a bond with Collin.

"You miss him, don't you?"

"Yeah."

"He misses you, too."

Mitch looked at her, hope as rich as the coffee-colored eyes. "You think?"

"I know. He told me on the phone last night." A phone call she'd instigated. Since the fire, he'd drawn back somewhat, as though he couldn't deal with all the emotions that had come pouring out that night. She was still puzzled and exhilarated by that unexpected kiss. Puzzled even more at how he had seemed to develop amnesia afterwards.

"He needs your help out there to get things going again. Let's call him later, huh?"

She would keep on calling until he opened up again.

"I guess so."

"Hey, Mitchell," Mia's dad called. "Are you going to sit around on the porch and suntan or are we going to that turkey shoot?"

"I'm ready." Mitchell leaped up, then caught himself and looked back at Mia. "Okay, Mia?"

After the fire she'd become Mia instead of Miss Carano. That kind of familiarity had never happened before with one of her clients, and she prayed she wouldn't lose perspective. Somehow Mitchell had wound his scruffy self around her heart and that of her family.

"Have fun."

Mitch was gone in a flash.

"You can depend on Dad to interrupt an important conversation," Rosalie murmured, coming to join Mia in Mitch's now-abandoned spot.

"Mitch needs the distraction. He's been pretty down since the fire."

"So have you. Maybe not down so much as too quiet. Want to talk about it?"

"I have a lot on my mind, Mama. That's all. Work, Mitch." She shrugged.

"Collin," Mama concluded.

"Yes. Him, too." She picked at a thread on her knit jacket. "He kissed me the night of the fire."

"Who could blame him? You're beautiful."

Mia laughed. "Oh, Mama, no wonder I love you so."

"You like him?"

"Maybe more than I should. I don't date guys who aren't Christians, Mom. You know that. You taught me that."

"But you're falling for him anyway."

Mia stared morosely at the crystal lights Adam and Nic were tacking in place along the board fence.

The brothers argued happily as they worked, the sound of frequent laughs punctuating the air. Two big ol' macho men with marshmallow hearts. How she loved them.

No wonder Collin Grace appealed to her. For all his outward toughness, he was a softie on the inside just like her brothers.

Two nights ago, he'd lost his hard facade, both with her and then later when he'd found the first of several dead animals. Happy, the little survivor, had saved himself. Mitchell had freed Panda and her remaining kittens, and the large animals were safe in outside pens. But one litter of new kittens and an old sickly dog and her pup hadn't made it out alive. Mia couldn't forget the look on Collin's face: stricken, haunted, guilty.

He'd looked the same in those seconds before he had kissed her. She couldn't get that look or that kiss off her mind.

A kiss shouldn't be such a big deal. She wasn't a teenager. But she had already been fighting her growing emotions and when he'd looked at her, fear and firelight in his eyes, and wrapped her in a hard, protective hug, she'd faced the hard truth. Christian or not, she had strong feelings for Collin Grace. And even if he never admitted it, Collin felt something for her, too. Maybe that's why he was running scared. Collin didn't like to feel.

The wind blew a lock of hair across her face. She pushed the curl behind one ear.

"At first, I thought I was helping Collin. You know, doing the Christian thing, being a witness, going the extra mile, trying to draw him out to a place where he can heal. Collin's a good man, Mama. But he's had so much heartache that he's afraid to trust anybody. Even God."

Mama took Mia's chilled hands in her warm ones. "Then our job is to show him that he can. That God is trustworthy. And so are we. Dad's trying to do that at the bakery."

"I know. After the fire I gave him a book to read, the one about finding your purpose through Christ. We talked about the Lord a little then, but I felt so inadequate in the face of what had happened. I'm not sure I said the right things. I wanted him to know that God cared about him and his animals and his losses."

She yearned to tell Mama about Collin's lost brothers and lean on her wisdom. But she'd promised confidentiality even though telling her mother would help both of them. Rosalie was a prayer warrior who never stopped praying for something until the answer came. Mia wasn't having much success on her own, but God knew where Ian and Drew were.

"How is he handling the fire?"

"The usual way—by pretending he isn't bothered." The fact that he'd retreated into his shell again told her the tough cop with the marshmallow center was mourning the animals and the uninsured barn.

If only she could find some trace of his brothers

to cheer him. Some bit of good news. She gripped her mother's hands tighter, giving them a quick bounce.

"Mama. I need you to help me pray about something."

Rosalie's eyes lit up. "Of course. What is it?"

"Well, that's the trouble. I need you to pray. But I can't tell you why."

Her mama looked at her for one beat of time, then smiled a mother's knowing smile. And Mia felt better than she'd felt since the night of the barn fire.

"Thank you, Lord," Mia said as she hung up the telephone. After going through dozens of boxes and hundreds of old records, she'd hit pay dirt two days after the conversation with her mama.

This time, she'd tempered her excitement long enough to make some phone calls and verify that a foster mother named Maxine Fielding not only still lived in Oklahoma City, but also remembered caring for a rowdy eleven-year-old named Drew Grace.

She glanced at the clock. Another two hours before she could head for Collin's place with her news. She thought about calling his cell, but found that unsatisfactory. She wanted to see his face, to watch him smile again. The past week had been a rough one.

A desk laden with paperwork needed her attention anyway, so she went to work there, weeding through files, making calls, setting up appointments. She phoned Mitchell's school to check on his attendance and discipline referrals and to inquire about any further indication of abuse.

Even with the barn fire setback, the boy had held his ground. And after the turkey shoot last Saturday, he'd let her take him out to Collin's where the three of them had spent hours putting together makeshift pens for the remaining animals.

The problems with the stepfather were accumulating though, and all her praying hadn't changed that one bit. The man had been furious when she'd interviewed him about Mitch's black eye, and Mitch hadn't helped by claiming he'd gotten into a fight at school. She wanted to get Mitch out of that house, though she couldn't without substantiated evidence. But now, both she and Collin were watching. Collin had even alerted the drug unit to be aware of possible illegal activities, though nothing had surfaced yet.

At ten after five she rotated her head from side to side, stretching tired muscles. Time to go. She tossed three Snickers wrappers into the trash and then dialed Collin's cell number.

"Grace."

She smiled at the short bark he substituted for a simple hello. And she couldn't deny that her heart jumped at the sound of that strong, masculine voice.

"Your name always makes me think of a song."

"Oh. Hi, Mia," he said. "I didn't recognize the number."

"My office."

"How does my name remind you of a song?"

She'd known he wouldn't let that one pass. With a smile in her voice, she said, "'*Amazing grace, how sweet the sound, that saved a wretch like me.*' It's a song about God's incredible love for us."

"The guys call me Amazing Grace sometimes. I never quite got that."

"Do you know what grace actually means?"

"I'm sure you're going to tell me." She heard the humor behind the gentle jab.

"Unmerited favor. God chooses to love and accept us, not because of what we do or don't do, but all because of His amazing grace."

A moment of silence hummed through the line. Though she hadn't planned to talk about her faith just now, she wanted Collin to understand how much Jesus loved him. She prayed that the truth of amazing grace would soak into his spirit and draw him to the Lord. She also hoped she hadn't just turned him ice-cold to the whole idea.

Finally, his voice soft, Collin said, "I'll never let the guys call me that again."

"Oh, Collin." He'd understood.

"So what's up?" he asked, sidestepping the emotion they both heard in her voice.

"I'm about to leave the office. Are you home?"

"Not yet. Why?"

"I want to talk to you in person."

"News?"

"Maybe." She didn't want to get his hopes up again and have them shattered.

"I'm off duty. Meet me at Braums on Penn. I'll buy you a grilled chicken salad."

"Throw in a hot chocolate and you've got yourself a date."

A soft masculine laugh flowed through the wires and straight into her heart. The memory of their kiss flared to life, unspoken but most definitely not forgotten. Oh, dear.

Mia bit down on the inside of her lip. Why couldn't she ever keep her big mouth shut?

Maxine Fielding had a great memory. The silver-haired woman regaled Collin with the good, the bad and the ugly about his brother's behavior. And the pleasure in Collin's face served as a reward for the lunch hours Mia had spent in the spooky, smelly basement of the municipal building.

"You don't by any chance have some pictures from that time, do you?" she asked the older woman. "Anything that could lead us to some of the boys who might have known Drew?"

"Sorry, hon," Maxine said, her fleshy face sorrowful. "I used to have a lot of pictures of my kids. That's what I always called them. Every one of them that came through here was mine for a while." She gestured with one hand. The knuckles were twisted with arthritis. "Anyways, while I was in the hospital a while back, my daughters decided to clean my house. Threw out all my mementos." She shook her head. "I'm still peeved about that."

Mia wished she hadn't asked, though Collin, sitting on an old velvet couch with his elbows on his knees, showed no emotion. His uniform was still neat after a day's work. And even with a five-o'clock shadow on his normally clean-shaven face, he looked good. A woman could get distracted with him around.

In fact, she *was* distracted. She let Collin do most of the talking, a strange turn of events. She was falling for him, all right, and didn't quite know what to do about it.

In the end, the foster mother recalled two other families that had cared for troubled boys during the same time period as well as a couple of group homes no longer in operation. That information alone gave Mia more names to plug into the computer, some specific files to dig through, and more chances to come up with something solid.

"So what do you think?" she asked when she and Collin were back inside his truck. He cranked the engine and pushed the heat lever to high. As night had fallen, so had the temperatures, and now a light rain spat at the windshield.

"Nice lady. I'm glad Drew was here for a while."

She could hear the unspoken wish that he'd been here, too. "Doesn't that give you hope that your brothers did okay in the system? That maybe they even found a family?"

"Wanna look into those locked files and find out?" A ghost of a smile reflected in the dashboard lights.

"No."

"I knew you'd say that." But his reply held humor instead of animosity, and she hoped he finally understood. There were some things she wouldn't do, even for him.

"Mrs. Fielding liked Drew."

"I've worried about him for so long, thought the worst." He shifted into Reverse and backed the truck onto the street. "Hearing that someone cared about him, even temporarily, felt good."

She was glad. More than glad, she was thankful. Collin had needed this news. He'd needed to leave the tragedy of the barn fire behind for a while. He'd needed to believe something positive had happened to his brothers. As he'd talked with Mrs. Fielding, he'd smiled, even laughed at her fond memories.

Collin's love for his lost brothers was fierce and steadfast, a powerful testament to the way he might someday love a woman. Mia refused to dwell on the lovely thought.

"We're going to find them, Collin."

He reached across the seat and touched her hand. "After tonight, I'm starting to believe you."

* * *

Three days before Thanksgiving the weather turned sunny and mild. Collin felt pretty sunny himself as he left the gym with his partner, Maurice, along with Adam Carano. The other two men argued amiably over which sit-ups worked best, straight knee or bent.

Adam had first come to the gym to discuss the lawsuit, but now he'd become a permanent member along with the two cops. Collin liked the guy. And he also admired the way Adam was handling the lawsuit. When he took on a case, he was a real bulldog. Like his sister.

Collin's smile widened. Thinking about Mia did that to him lately.

"What are you grinning about, Grace?" Adam slapped him on the back. Collin's sweat-damp sweat-shirt stuck to his shoulder.

"You talk as much as your sister."

"That's a terrible thing to say to your lawyer."

"When are you going to quit torturing me and get that problem solved?"

"I'm getting close. Did you know your neighbor has a real problem with cops? Especially you?"

Collin sawed a towel back and forth behind his neck. "Tell me something I don't already know."

"Okay, I will." Adam looked pleased with himself. "You remember busting a kid named Joey Stapleton a few years back for breaking and entering?"

"No, but the fire inspector suspects my barn was arson. Not B and E." His good mood evaporated at the memory of the animals Mia, Mitch and he had buried beneath the harvest moon.

Adam held up a hand. "Collin, my man. Lesson one about attorney-client privileges. Never interrupt your lawyer when he's on a roll. You disappoint me. You didn't even ask how Stapleton was connected."

"Okay, I'll bite. Who is he?"

"First of all, Stapleton didn't burn down your barn. He's still serving time. However, his half-brother, who mortgaged his land to defend Stapleton, lives down the road from you. His name is Cecil Slokum."

Now that *was* interesting. But there were plenty of do-wrongs out there with a grudge against him. "You think Slokum could be responsible?" Collin asked.

"Maybe. If Slokum can force you to pay damages for his daughter's ewe and destroy your barn at the same time, he not only gets revenge, he gets back some of the money he spent on his so-called innocent brother."

Collin had entertained the thought before, but a man didn't accuse his neighbor of arson without some kind of evidence. He'd also suspected Mitch of the fire and had lived to regret that mistake. Though his young friend was hanging around the farm once more, Collin could feel a hesitancy in the relationship, as though Mitch feared Collin would turn on him again.

"You got evidence?"

"Circumstantial, but enough to strongly suspect."

Collin's jaw tightened. Though he wanted to grab Cecil Slokum by the neck and shake the truth out of him, he wouldn't. He wasn't that kind of cop.

"Where do we go from here? Anything we can bust him on?"

"I've turned my findings over to the fire marshal and the DA. If I'm right—" Adam's grin was cocky "—and I usually am, an arrest could come at any time."

"I appreciate it." Although sincere, Collin heard the gruffness in the thanks. He wasn't a lawyer and couldn't do the job Adam could, but he didn't like needing anyone's help either. More and more lately, Adam and Mia and the whole Carano clan made him feel needy. Inside and out. It kept him off balance, edgy, vulnerable.

"I can't believe I didn't figure out Cecil's grudge myself." In fact, he was annoyed that he hadn't dug deeper when the suspicion first sprouted. But work and Mitchell and rebuilding, not to mention Mia and his search, had kept him too busy to think straight.

"That's what friends are for, Collin. To lighten the load."

The words *unmerited favor* flitted through his mind. Was that what Mia meant? He'd thought a lot about that conversation, and the idea that anyone would do something for him without expecting anything in return never would jibe.

"How much do I owe you?" he asked.

Adam looked at him, an odd smile on his face. "My sister would hurt me if I took your money."

A cord of tension wound around inside him. Cool from drying sweat and November air, he shrugged into his hoodie. "I pay my debts."

"There are some debts you can't pay, Collin. The sooner you learn that the better off you'll be. The better off my sister will be, too."

Collin had no clue what Adam meant. And he didn't think he wanted to ask. Especially about the reference to Mia.

They were nearing his truck, and he needed this settled now. "How much, Carano?"

Adam rubbed a hand over his chin as if in deep thought. "Tell you what, Grace. If you really want to repay me, you can do me a favor."

"Name it."

Too late, Collin saw the ornery twinkle.

"Come to Mama's house for Thanksgiving dinner."

Maurice started to laugh. His partner knew his aversion to large family gatherings. He'd also been on Collin's case about Mia.

"I think he blindsided you, partner."

Adam shrugged his wide shoulders and didn't look the least bit sorry. "What do you expect? Lawyers are supposed to be sneaky." He pointed a finger at Collin. "You're going to show up, aren't you?"

"Do I have a choice?"

"Actually, no." Then, with a laugh and a wave,

Adam hopped into a sleek SUV and left him standing in the parking lot. To make matters worse, Maurice was still laughing.

## *Chapter Eleven*

Anticipation, sweeter than Christmas morning, filled Mia. She'd had so many failures, but today she felt sure something new would turn up in this stack of records.

With Mrs. Fielding's information, she had located the placement files of the family that had taken Drew after he'd run away from the Fielding home. Surely some mention of Collin's brother would be inside this folder.

She rummaged in her desk for a Snickers, but after a glance at her dusty hands, changed her mind. With the holidays coming up, she'd be fighting more than five pounds if she wasn't careful.

She flipped through page after page, eyes straining at the faded typewritten print until some of her excitement began to fade. The records seemed jumbled, bits and pieces of several files that might or might not relate to Collin's brothers. Then, as if lit by a neon sign, Drew's name leaped out at her.

"Yes!" she whispered, barely able to contain her excitement.

Collin knew she and Mama were praying for a breakthrough, and he'd been politely receptive, but Mia was ready for God to show off a little and prove to Collin that prayer really worked.

She quickly perused the document, found nothing of significance and decided to put the sheet aside while she searched for others. If there was one page about him, perhaps there would be more.

But when she reached the bottom of a rather thick file, two yellowing forms was all she had found. Disappointed, but not disheartened, she settled back to read, hoping for any tidbit to share with Collin.

One was a general report concerning the reasons Drew continued to live in foster care. There was a chronicle of his psycho-social problems, his habit of skipping school, and numerous reports for fighting. He'd been removed from any number of places because of the chip on his shoulder and his propensity for running away.

The other was a social worker's report indicating a placement in a therapeutic group home with six other teenage boys. Her heart fell into her high heels. Drew was fifteen at that point and had been in foster care since age seven. Gone was any hope that he had found a forever family.

She stopped to rub her tired eyes. Thirty was creeping closer and she'd always heard the eyes were the first to go. She needed to schedule a checkup with her optometrist—soon.

After jotting down names and addresses that might prove useful she started to replace the folder in the appropriate box when a newspaper clipping slipped out and filtered to the floor.

The word *fire* caught her attention. Her heart thumped once, hard. The reaction was silly, she told herself. A newspaper article about a fire wasn't necessarily about Drew.

But the clipping *had* been in the same file.

Unable to shake the foreboding, Mia picked up the two-inch column and read. A fire had broken out in a foster home claiming the lives of several teens, though no names were mentioned.

Dread, heavy as a grand piano, came over her. The address matched one of the homes that had cared for Drew. And the timing was perfect.

She rifled through the box, hoping to find something more about the tragedy but came up empty. Finally, she rested her chin in her hand and stared at the clipping, unsure of what to do with this new information. Should she tell Collin right away? Or keep the clipping to herself until she could verify whether Drew had been in that fire?

She rubbed at her eyes again. This time they were moist.

* * *

Collin stood in the doorway watching Mia. Deeply focused on her work, she hadn't heard him come in.

Her dark auburn hair swung forward, brushing her cheek, grazing the top of her desk. He studied her, remembering the silkiness of that hair, the softness of her skin.

He couldn't escape the memory of that night. Especially that insane moment when he'd kissed her and she'd kissed him back. More than once, he'd been tempted to repeat the performance, but caution won out. She pretended nothing incredible had happened. So would he. But that didn't stop him thinking about it.

Her mouth was turned down tonight, unusual for Mia. She rubbed at the corner of one eye and sighed. She was tired.

Her regular workload was always heavy and she was involved in church and the community, but for the past few months, she had been committed to helping him and Mitch. In her spare time, if there was such a thing, she searched the records for his brothers. In the evenings, she was now an active participant, along with Mitch, in rebuilding the barn. He'd asked too much of her.

He was suddenly overcome with a fierce need to take the load off her shoulders. To cheer her up. To make her laugh. Mia had a great laugh.

"Got a minute?"

Mia jumped and slapped one hand over her heart. Her red-rimmed eyes widened. "Collin."

"Didn't mean to scare you." He stepped inside the small office.

"What's wrong?" She didn't smile her usual wide, happy welcome.

"Why does anything have to be wrong?" Man, she was pretty, even with her hair mussed and her eyes red and every bit of makeup rubbed away.

"Because you hate this place. You never come here." She didn't look all that happy to see him.

He frowned. What was going on with her tonight? "Want me to leave?"

She rotated her head from side to side, stretching tight muscles. Collin thought about offering a neck rub, but decided against it. Last time he'd touched her, he'd gone nuts and kissed her, too.

"Don't be silly."

Which was no answer at all. He shifted from one foot to the other and checked out the messy office. Boxes, bent and aging, lined one wall and stacks of manila folders with glaring white typewritten labels were spread here and there.

"Are these the old records you've been searching for me?"

A funny expression flitted across her face. For a second, he wondered if she'd found something. But if she had, wouldn't she be shouting from the rooftops and talking a mile a minute? Instead, she was abnormally quiet tonight.

"These are only a few of the hundreds and hundreds of boxes in that basement," she said.

"Maybe I could help." His offer should have come long before now, but he suspected the files were confidential.

Mia shook her head, long hair swishing over the shoulders of a bright-blue sweater. Blue was definitely her color.

"I was about to stop for the night anyway." She slid some papers into a folder and looked up at him. "So are you going to tell me why you're here or can I assume I'm under arrest?"

This time she offered a smile.

This was the Mia he knew and…appreciated.

"I came with some news." He scraped a straight-backed chair up closer to her desk and sat down. "Unless Adam beat me to it."

Her smile disappeared and she tensed again. "What kind of news? Did something happen?"

Collin waved away her concern. "Nothing bad. At least, I hope you don't think so. Adam invited me to your Mom's for Thanksgiving."

She studied him for two beats. "So did I, but you said no."

That wasn't the reaction he'd anticipated.

"I'm coming now."

"What changed your mind?"

"Your brother is a devious man."

He expected her to laugh and agree. She didn't. She seemed distracted, not really into the conversation. Earlier he'd felt unwanted, but now he saw what he hadn't before. Something was wrong.

He leaned across the desk to tug at her hand. The bones felt small and fine, and her skin was smoother and softer than Happy's fur. "Let's get out of here. You're exhausted."

"It's not that, Collin. Oh, I am tired, but I'm also upset about something I found in an old file. I need to tell you and I'm not sure how."

That got his attention. The desire to tease her about Thanksgiving dinner disappeared. "Whose old files are we talking about?"

"Drew's. Or at least files associated with Drew. There's some confusion in them. Several files seem to be jumbled together with parts missing. Maybe a box was spilled somehow and hastily repacked. I don't know. But I did find some information that may or may not involve Drew."

He saw the pinched skin around her mouth, the worry around her eyes. And he knew beyond a shadow of a doubt, the news was not going to make him happy.

The day before Thanksgiving Collin unearthed an ancient police report which identified the cause of the Carter Home fire as an electrical short. Better yet, the report listed several witnesses, one of whom turned out to be another former foster kid, Billy Johnson. Collin needed less than thirty minutes to track down the man's name, address and place of employment.

"I'm going with you," Mia said, when he called to tell her of the discovery.

"This is your day off. I thought you and your mom were cooking."

"We are. We still can. But I'm going with you. Don't argue. Come pick me up."

Collin hid a smile. Deep down, he was glad that the bulldog in Mia insisted on going along. Something in him worried that the interview might produce bad news. And though Mia couldn't stop bad news, she was a dandy with moral support and comforting prayers. He'd come to respect that about her. He'd even tried praying a few times himself lately.

Someone had died in that house fire. That's when he'd started praying in earnest. Praying that Drew wasn't the one. He'd even taken to bargaining with God. If Drew was alive, he would believe. If Drew was okay, God must care. He knew such prayers were selfish and unfruitful, but he was a desperate man.

Billy Johnson met them in the grease bay of an auto repair shop on the east side of town, a rag in hand. His blue service uniform was streaked with oil and grease and his fingernails would never see clean, but when he offered his hand, Collin shook it gratefully. This man had known Drew at age fifteen.

"Kinda cold out here," Billy said. "Y'all come inside the office. My boss won't care. I told him you were coming."

They followed the mechanic inside the tiny office stacked with tools and papers and red rags and reeking of grease. A small space heater kept the room pleasantly warm.

"Y'all have a seat." He shoved a car-repair manual off one chair and swiped the red rag over the seat for Mia. Collin settled onto a canvas camp stool. No one sat around this place much.

"I remember Drew." Billy rolled a stool from beneath the desk and balanced on it, pushing himself back and forth with one extended foot. "He was a wiry rascal. Liked to fight."

Collin shot Mia a wry glance. "Sounds like my brother."

"He was okay, though. Me and him, we only punched each other once. After that, we was kinda buddies, ya might say." He grinned. "Foster kids, ya know. We sneaked smokes together. Raided the kitchen. Tormented the house parents. The usual."

"What do you remember about the night of the fire?" Mia asked, and Collin was grateful. His shoulder muscles were as tight as security at the White House. He wanted to get this over with.

"More than I want to," Billy said, scratching at the back of his head. The metal rollers on his stool made an annoying screech against the cement floor. "The house was full, seven or eight boys, I think, so I was asleep in the living room on the couch when the fire broke out."

"But you woke in time to escape?"

"Yes, ma'am. Me and this one other kid." He rolled the stool in and out, in and out, oblivious to the screech.

"Was it Drew?"

"No, ma'am." *Screech. Screech.* "A kid named Jerry. I think he's in the pen now."

Blood pulsing against his temples, Collin leaned forward. "What about Drew?"

Billy hesitated. Collin got a real bad feeling, worse than the time he'd walked into a dark alley and come face to face with a double-barrelled shotgun.

The screeching stopped. "Drew slept in the attic. I'm sorry, officer. Your brother never made it out."

Mia wanted Collin to get angry. She wanted him to cry. She wanted him to react in some way, to show some emotion. But he didn't.

With his cop face on, he thanked Billy Johnson and quietly led the way to the car. The drive back to Mia's apartment was unbearable. She talked, muttered maddeningly useless platitudes, said she was sorry a million times, reminded him that Ian was still out there somewhere, but Collin said nothing in response.

"Why don't you come inside for a while?" she asked when he stopped outside her apartment. "I'll make us something to eat. Better yet, my tiramisu brownies are already baked for tomorrow's dinner. We can sneak one with some fresh coffee. I know brownies and coffee won't change things, but comfort food always makes me feel better."

"I don't think so."

Her heart broke for him. Lord, hasn't he had enough sorrow in his life? Why this?

She pushed the door open, hesitant to leave him alone. "Will you call me later if you need to talk?"

For a minute, she thought he might respond, might even smile. He'd teased her so many times about her tendency to rattle on, but this time he was hurting too much even to tease.

"I'll come out to your place later if you want me to. Or you can come back here. You really shouldn't be alone."

He looked at her and what she read there was clearer than words and so terribly sad she wanted to cry. He'd always been alone.

"I'm here for you, Collin. If you need anything at all, please call me. Let me help. I don't know what to do either, but I want to do something."

Feeling helpless, she slid out of the truck and stood with one hand holding the door open. Wind swirled around her legs, chilling her. Someone slammed an apartment door and pounded down the metal stairs outside her complex.

"I'm praying for you, Collin. God cares. I care. My family cares. Please know that."

This time he answered, his voice low, and Mia thought she saw a crack in the hard veneer. "I do know."

She couldn't help herself. She reached back inside the cab and touched his cheek. Her heart was full of sorrow and love and the desire to help him heal, but this time she was the one with no words.

Collin reached up and took her hand from his whisker-rough face, gave it a squeeze and let go. "Better get inside. You'll freeze."

She backed away, reluctant to let him leave, but having no other choice.

"We'll see you tomorrow at Mama's, won't we?"

"I don't know, Mia," he said. "I probably wouldn't be very good company."

And then he drove away.

# *Chapter Twelve*

*Dead.*

The word clattered round and round in Collin's head like a rock in an empty pop can.

Drew, his full-of-energy-and-orneriness brother, was dead. Long dead.

All the years of searching, hoping, gone up in smoke in a house where the kids were throwaways that nobody wanted anyway. Nobody missed them. Nobody mourned them.

He lay on his bed in the darkness, staring up at the shadows cast by the wind-tossed maple outside his window. He had used all the energy in him to drive home and care for the animals. By the time he'd dragged his heavy heart inside, he hadn't had the energy to undress except for his boots.

He'd been alone for years, but tonight he felt

empty as if part of him had disappeared. In a way, he supposed it had. The search for his brothers had sustained him since he was ten years old. The hope of reunion had kept him moving forward, kept him fighting upstream when he'd been ready to give up on life in general. The search had given him purpose, made him a cop. Now, half of that hope was gone forever. And with it, half of himself.

He heard the soft shuffle of animal feet on wood floors. The familiar limp and thump that could only belong to Happy.

After the fire, Collin hadn't had the heart to leave the little guy outside with the others. So Happy had moved into a box in the living room, quietly filling Collin's evenings with his sweet presence.

But now, he whined at the bedside, an unusual turn of events.

"What do you want, boy?" Collin said to the dark ceiling.

Happy whined again.

Though his body weighed a thousand pounds and moving took effort he didn't have, Collin rolled to his side and peered down at the shadowy form. The collie lifted one footless leg and pawed at him. When Collin didn't pick him up, Happy tried to jump, a pitiful sight that sent the dog tumbling backwards.

Collin swooped him up onto the bed. "Here now."

With a contented sigh, Happy buried his nose under his master's arm and settled down. Collin had never had a dog. Not as a pet. But Happy was getting real close. Both his legs had finally healed after the second amputation, but a dog with two missing feet wasn't likely ever to be adopted.

He smoothed his hand over the shaggy fur, glad for the company of another creature, especially one that didn't talk.

No, that wasn't fair. He liked Mia to talk. He loved her soothing, sweet voice. He loved her enthusiasm for life, her positive take on everything, her belief in the ultimate goodness. She was a light in a dark place.

Mia had been so upset for him. He'd wanted to talk to her, wanted to let her help, but he couldn't. He didn't know how.

Burrowing one hand deep into Happy's thick fur, Collin drew comfort from the warm, loving dog.

A lot of good prayer had done. Not that he expected God to pay any attention to him. But Mia had prayed. And if God was going to listen to anybody, wouldn't He hear someone like her?

With his free hand, Collin dug down into his pants' pocket, felt the metal fish. All this time he'd carried the keychain as a reminder of his brothers. Of that last day together. Of the counselor who'd prayed for them and shown them kindness, given them hope. Had Drew still carried his that fateful night?

A fire. Another fire. He squeezed his eyes shut, but quickly opened them when flames shot up behind his imagination. Drew in a fire. Helpless. Just like the animals in his barn.

All night, he lay there, unable to sleep, unable to stop picturing the burned animals he'd had to bury. Unable to stop his imagination from making the terrible comparison.

When at last the sun broke above the horizon, heralding the new day, Collin rolled onto his belly and pulled the pillow over his head.

Today was Thanksgiving.

And he wasn't feeling too thankful.

At noon Collin awakened, cold and depressed, to a very urgent demand from Happy to be let outside. Amazed to have slept at all, he stumbled to the front door, bleary-eyed and heavy-headed. The house was cold and the wood floors chilled his bare feet. He'd forgotten to turn on the heat last night.

After cranking the thermostat, he stood at the door to watch the collie hobble around the front yard, tail in motion, sniffing the scent of the resident squirrel as if he had the legs to catch it. Collin had to admit, the little dog's attitude had a positive effect on his own.

When Happy made the choice to stay outside and play, Collin closed the door and went to make coffee.

He felt bad about backing out of dinner at the Caranos'. He didn't like disappointing Mia—or any of the others for that matter. They were a great family. The best. The kind he would have loved to have grown up in. But he didn't belong, especially not today when negative energy was all he had to share.

He hoped Mitch was there, though, instead of at home. The boy needed the Caranos.

While the coffee brewed, the kitchen grew warmer, but Collin's feet didn't. He headed for the bedroom in search of clean socks.

As he opened the dresser drawer, his attention fell to the book Mia had given to him the night of the barn fire. She'd said the contents would encourage him, help him understand his purpose. Until yesterday he'd believed his purpose was to find his brothers. Now he wondered if there had to be more to life than a single-minded effort to accomplish only one thing. He'd found Drew, for whatever good that had done him. What would he do after he found Ian? Once his only purpose was fulfilled, then what? Would his life be over?

Without giving the decision too much thought, he grabbed the book along with a pair of socks and headed for the kitchen and that much-needed cup of coffee. The smell alone was waking him up.

He poured a cup and sat down at the table, flipped the book to a random page, and began to read.

Late that afternoon Happy's excited yip warned Collin that he was not alone. He jammed his hammer into the loop on his tool belt and walked around to the front of the house. For the last few hours, he'd sweated out his depression on the house-in-progress while mulling over the things he'd read in Mia's book.

As he stood in the front yard, chilled by winter wind on sweat, a caravan of familiar-looking vehicles wound down his driveway, stirred dry leaves and dust and elicited a cacophony of barking from the penned dogs. Happy danced on two feet and a pair of stubs, furry tail in overdrive, mouth stretched into a wide smile.

One fist propped on his hip, Collin blinked in bewilderment at the incoming traffic. Mia's yellow Mustang led the pack, an entire invasion of Caranos.

"Hi Collin." Mitch jumped out of Mia's barely stopped car, wearing new jeans and an oversize OU jersey. Happy was all over him like honey glaze on ham, wiggling and whining, eyes aglow with love. Mitch laughed in delight and fell to the ground, pulling the dog onto his chest.

Adam bolted out of his red SUV and came charging across the yard, a mock scowl on his face. "Hey, squirt. Don't be desecrating my OU jersey like that."

Mitch leaped up, brushing away the dust. "Sorry, Adam."

Mitchell had come a long way from the defiant kid Collin had picked up for shoplifting.

Adam ruffled his head. "Joking. The jersey is yours. I told you that." He stuck a hand out toward Collin, his dark eyes sparking with the Carano humor. "As your lawyer, I have an obligation to tell you something." He jerked his head toward the rest of the laughing, jabbering group who came toward the house loaded with boxes and dishes. "These women cooked a mega-meal. And any invited man who doesn't show up to eat it could be in serious danger."

"What is all this?"

"You know the old saying. If Mohammed won't come to the mountain, the mountain will come to him. So, the Caranos have moved Thanksgiving to your place."

"You're kidding." Collin stared in amazement as the whole group trouped inside his house. A waft of incredibly delicious smells trailed them.

Adam clapped him on the back. "Caranos take their food seriously. Especially Thanksgiving food."

The old feelings of inadequacy crowded in with the unexpected company. His house was tiny and his table impossibly small. How would they have a dinner inside there? How would they all even get inside?

But the undaunted Carano clan had thought of everything. From the back of a pickup came folding tables and chairs. He watched, unmoving for several long, bewildered minutes while all around him people laughed and joked and juggled boxes and covered dishes. Why had they done this? Why would Mia and her family go to so much trouble to bring Thanksgiving to a guy who was accustomed to having no holidays at all? Why did they care?

"Close your mouth, Collin," Mia said as she

swished past him smelling like sunshine and banana nut bread. "And take this into the house."

Her smile warmed a cold place inside him.

He accepted the foil-wrapped package, still warm from the oven. "You didn't have to do this."

She pointed a finger at him. "Don't say that to Mama."

He didn't understand this kind of family bond. He didn't understand these people. They scared him and nurtured him and made him long to be someone he wasn't. He didn't know whether to run away from them or to them.

For today, he figured he didn't have much say in the matter either way. If this was a game of tag, you're it, he was it. Might as well make the best of the situation.

The twenty-odd people were a tight fit inside Collin's home-in-progress, requiring some creative arrangement, but in no time at all his house smelled of the huge Thanksgiving dinner spread out before them on folding tables. Someone, Mia, he figured, had even thought of brown-and-orange tablecloths and a perky tissue-turkey centerpiece.

Around him, conversation ebbed and flowed. Nic, wearing a sweatshirt that proclaimed *I'm going to graduate on time no matter how long it takes,* wielded a carving knife and fork with a maniacal laugh that had the girls squealing.

As he watched the interaction of people who

loved each other, some of the heavy sorrow lifted from Collin. Every time he hung out with the Caranos, he was overwhelmed with both yearning and fear. Yearning to be a part. Fear that he didn't have what it took.

He removed a stack of plates from Mia's hands and began to set them out in long rows.

"I hope you aren't upset with our invasion," Mia said, her sweet eyes seriously concerned that he was angry with her. "I couldn't stand to think of you out here alone on Thanksgiving."

He'd figured Mia was the instigator. She had wanted to be here—with him—and the idea gave him a happy little buzz. Maybe he had it in him after all.

Dinner was over, but the pleasant zing of having Mia and her family in his house didn't go away. The television blared a game between the Lions and the Cowboys which brought occasional shouts of victory from Adam and Nic. Gabe and his wife were deep into a game of Go Fish with their oldest child while the youngest was fast asleep in Collin's bedroom. Mitchell was sprawled with his back against Leo's knees, Happy in his lap. They all looked as full and drowsy and content as Collin felt.

*Contentment* was not a word he used very often. But something had happened to him today when Mia's family had come onto his turf to draw him into their midst with food and love. If he dwelled on the idea, he'd probably get nervous and back off, so he chose to enjoy. His mind needed their exuberant distraction.

"I'm on KP," he said, gently nudging Rosalie out from in front of his shiny stainless-steel sink. "Cleaning up is the least I can do."

A chorus of groans issued from the Carano men.

"Traitor," Nic grumbled.

"You're starting a terrible precedent," Adam called. "Next year, they'll expect us to cook."

This time the women hooted.

"Anna and I will help Collin, Mama. There's really not room for more than three, anyway. You go sit down. You've cooked for three days."

"Sounds good. I wanted to watch this game anyway." Rosalie untied her apron and hung the starched poplin over the back of a chair. "When these tables are cleared, you boys get them folded and put out in the truck so we have room to play charades or something."

"Will do, Mama."

Rosalie bustled around the tables and squeezed a chair into a tiny space between the wall and Leo. Collin leaned toward Mia and murmured, "Your mom likes football?"

Mia looked up from scraping leftover yams into a container and grinned. He loved the way she always had a smile ready to share. "Mama doesn't know a touchdown from a field goal, but she treasures the time with her boys."

"Your family's lucky to have her."

Mia studied him, expression soft and understanding. "We're very blessed."

Blessed. Yeah, he could see that. But they worked at being a family, too. At this whole togetherness thing. They were a clear picture of how functional families made it happen. Sacrifice, commitment, overlooking each other's quirks. He understood that now in a way he hadn't before.

"I'll wash. You dry. Dishtowels in that top drawer." He took a heavy ceramic dish from her and dumped the empty bowl into the soapy water. "You Caranos are great cooks. I can't believe I ate two pieces of pie."

Mia reached for a rinsed glass and their arms brushed. Suddenly, he was remembering that disconcerting kiss.

"There's more for later."

He'd like that a lot. And he didn't mean pie.

They made short work of the kitchen, Anna and Mia whisking dishes and leftovers from the tables while he scrubbed away. While the women carried on most of the conversation Collin listened, comfortable with their chatter.

"I think that's the last one," Mia said, taking a huge stainless pot from his drippy hands.

Collin looked around, saw the tables cleared, and pulled the plug. "Good. The animals are probably thinking I've abandoned them. Can you take over from here?"

"I can," Anna said, her smile a mirror of Mia's. "You two go on. I'll finish up and make some fresh coffee, too."

"I'm not arguing with a deal like that," Mia said.

Nic popped up from his folding chair as Collin and Mia donned their coats. "Need any help?"

"We've got it. Thanks, anyway." As much as he liked Nic and the other Caranos, he was ready to be alone. Well, almost alone.

Collin pushed the storm door open and waited for Mia to pass through. Her companionship no longer felt like an intrusion. He figured he should worry about that. Later.

Once outside he was tempted, if only for a split second, to take her hand. He settled for a hand under her elbow instead. A man had to form some kind of boundaries with a woman like Mia.

As they fell into step toward the lean-to that now served as shelter for the remaining animals, she glanced over at him. "You didn't get much sleep last night."

"Perceptive." Beneath a narrow slice of silver moon, the air had grown frosty. Collin's breath puffed out beneath the bright yard light. Last night had been one of the worst nights of his life.

"The bags under your eyes gave you away." She slowed her steps to rest one hand on his upper arm. Whether imagined or real, Mia's warmth penetrated the sleeve of his thick coat. "How are you? Really."

"Better now." That surprised him. To know that family not his own could lift his spirits this much.

"I'm so sorry. Deeply, truly sorry. You have every right to be angry and hurt and grief-stricken. I wish I knew what to do to make things better."

She already had. She and her rambunctious family with their big hearts and their open arms.

"Every holiday for more than twenty years, I've wondered about my brothers. I know what happened to Drew now, but what about Ian? Does he have a family to go home to? A wife and kids? Is he having turkey and dressing and pumpkin pie right this minute with a loving family?"

*Or is he as lonely and messed up as me?*

"We're going to keep on believing and praying that he's okay and that we are going to locate him. If we found information about Drew, we can find Ian."

"I hope you're right." Maybe then the hole inside him would heal a little.

As they approached the pens, the animals moved restlessly, eager for their own Thanksgiving dinner. The colt whinnied a greeting. A cat meowed, followed by a chorus of kitten mews.

Even after losing six animals to the fire and making the decision to take no more until the barn was rebuilt, he still had too many animals. Caged up this way was no life for them and he hated the arrangement, though there was no other place for the strays to go. He'd ruled out the animal shelter knowing that sick animals wouldn't be adopted and the alternative was euthanasia. Better with him than there. Some were well enough to move around inside a stall but not well enough to be safe from coyotes and other predators if he left them loose. The puppies and kittens were in borrowed cages that opened out to short, makeshift runs. The larger dogs were on chains next to borrowed dog houses. The grazing animals were the lucky ones, unaffected by the fire except for the loss of stall space.

He went to the row of barrels that contained a variety of animal feed. "I have to find a way to get this barn up faster."

At the rate he was going, the barn wouldn't be finished for a year. He had only one stall completed to house the sickest, and a chain-link run for the dogs.

Mia began to distribute dry dog food, stopping to give each animal an ear rub. "I'll feed everyone while you take care of the medications."

He gave her a grateful look. "Good idea."

Panda, who had survived the fire and recovered sufficiently to be adopted, had yet to find a home, though her kittens had. Collin figured he'd never find a place for her. The mama cat allowed Collin or Mia to feed her, but otherwise she feared humans except for Mitchell.

"I thought this was Mitchell's job," Mia said, coming around the shadowy side of the lean-to.

Collin knelt on the ground dabbing antibiotic cream onto a pup's stitches. "He's through serving his time."

"I know. But the responsibility has been good for him."

"He's changed a lot."

"Thanks to you." She handed him a roll of adhesive tape.

"And your family. Sometimes I wonder what will happen to him."

"His stepdad scares me."

Collin looked at her sharply. She'd shoved her hands into her pockets. "Do you mean personally or professionally?"

Even in the halflight, he saw her frown. "Both. Since you told me of your suspicions, I want Mitch out of there, but…"

"But Mitch won't tell you the truth." He put the finishing touches on the bandage and stood. He was as frustrated as Mia over Mitch's reluctance to give them a reason to move him to safety. And for all his watchfulness, Collin couldn't find reasonable cause to pay Teddy Shipley an unexpected official visit.

"I think Mitch won't talk because his mother is using, too. He's afraid of what will happen to her."

In his entire life, including twelve years on the force, Collin had seen nothing but horror come from drugs. He was lucky. Mia would say blessed. And maybe he was. Whichever, he'd somehow escaped the trap of drugs. Too many of the boys he'd known in the group homes were dead, in jail, or living lives of unspeakable despair because of drugs.

"If a meth lab is operating in that house, it's only a matter of time until something bad goes down."

Her voice was stunned. "Do you think that's the case?"

"Maybe." Probably. They were gathering more evidence daily.

A chill of fear trickled down his backbone. "Stay out of there, Mia. You hear me?"

"I'm afraid for him, Collin."

"Me, too," he admitted grimly. Collin knew the reality of Mitchell's situation. Mia was an experienced professional, but she hadn't lived the life. He had.

In silence, his thoughts churning, he put the medical supply box away and doubled-checked the cage latches for security. He couldn't keep the whole world safe, but he could take care of these animals. And Mitchell, too, if the kid would only let him.

Mia tugged on the front of his coat. Her hair blew softly back from her face as she looked up at him. "Stop fretting. You can't always be with him. But Jesus is."

"'He'll never leave you nor forsake you,'" he quoted softly, the words of his keychain making more sense at that moment than they ever had.

"Exactly."

If he was indeed blessed to have avoided the curse of drugs, was Jesus the reason? Had God been with him through everything? "Do you think it's true?"

"I know it is." She pulled her hood up and shivered against a sudden gust of wind.

Collin draped an arm around her shoulders and drew her against his side. She fitted beneath his arm as if curved in exactly the right places for that purpose.

They started back toward the house. Collin reined in his long stride to accommodate her shorter one.

"Mind if I ask you something?" His words were deep and thoughtful.

"Anything." And she meant it.

"I can't believe how much I've laughed tonight."

She bumped him with her hip. "That's not a question."

"After hearing about Drew—" He stopped. Talking about his brother's death was still too fresh and cut too deep.

Mia slipped an arm around his waist and squeezed. She prayed he could feel her compassion and somehow gain comfort. From the time she and Adam had come up with the idea to bring Thanksgiving to him, she'd prayed. Thankfully, he'd responded well to their invasion and had even seemed to enjoy himself in spite of the awful sorrow in his heart.

"I want to ask you something," he said, stopping in a wind break next to the front porch. From inside the house Mia could hear one of the first Christmas commercials of the season.

"Sounds serious."

"It is. I've spent most of my adult life coming to terms with my crazy life, but I'll never understand Drew's death. That's where I'm confused about God. I want to believe He cares but the evidence isn't too strong. I don't mean I'm angry at Him or that I blame Him. But He doesn't seem too involved in my life so far."

His words were not bitter. Instead, they held a yearning, a seeking to understand. Somehow in all the past rejections, Collin had come to see himself as unlovable.

Mia looked up at him, at the strong, manly profile illuminated by the moon. She admired so much about Collin Grace that he didn't even recognize as good. He'd overcome some incredible odds to become a man with so much depth of character, so much rich emotion that he didn't know how to express all that was inside him.

She shifted against the wall and gazed off into the darkness, praying for wisdom. She'd been a Christian since she was twelve years old. She had a strong, healthy family and many friends. Though she'd had hurts and struggles, nothing in her experience could compare to what this good and decent man had lived through. How could she make him understand that God was here, caring? How could she make him understand that he was loved and loveable?

Her heart filled with realization. Tonight was the night he needed to know.

"I don't have any easy answers. I wish I did. But there's something I want to share with you. Actually, three somethings."

Collin peered down at her, his expression sincere and curious. She saw a trust there that gave her courage.

"First of all, I don't pretend to understand why terrible things happen to innocent people, especially kids. But I do know that God cares. So much that He sent His son to give us hope of a better place than this. A perfect place called Heaven.

"Secondly, He knew Drew's death would devastate you. He kept the news from you until you were ready to handle it. Until you had met a crazy bunch of Caranos who would try their best to help you through the grief."

"Why didn't he just give me back my brother? That's the only thing I've ever wanted."

"I don't know, Collin. I wish He had. But God has a plan for you. And even if Drew isn't a part of your future, he'll always be a part of who you are and what you've become—a good cop, a caring man, a dear and trusted friend."

A gust of wind whipped her hood back. Collin caught each side and tugged the hood up around her face. When she thanked him with a half smile, he moved a fraction closer.

Mia's skin tingled from his nearness. As hard as this was going to be, she had to tell him the truth—all of it.

In the narrow space between them, her breath mingled with his, moist and warm. They really should go inside.

She could see he wanted to kiss her again. And she wanted that too, but she wouldn't follow through. The first time had been unplanned reflex, completely understandable and forgivable. This time would be premeditated.

"Wasn't there a third thing you wanted to tell me?" he murmured, wonderfully, painfully near.

She wasn't scared of the truth, but she didn't know how to predict Collin's reaction. Was she doing the right thing by telling him? She fidgeted with the string on her hood but held Collin's gaze with hers. His expression might not change, but his eyes would tell her what he wouldn't.

"Yes. There is. Something very important. Something that I hope will make you realize how special and valuable you are. At least to me."

Inside the house, Nic's voice shouted "Touchdown!" Neither she nor Collin reacted.

She had his full attention now.

Throat thick with emotion, Mia bracketed Collin's

face in her gloved hands. And then, her voice sure, she said, "The third thing is this: I'm in love with you, Collin."

# Chapter Thirteen

Collin blinked into her eyes, stunned. She loved him?

A thousand responses thundered through him as wild as mustangs. He didn't know what she expected him to say. He had feelings for her, wanted to kiss her, to be with her, but love? He wasn't even sure what that was.

"You don't have to respond to that." She gave his jaws a final caress and dropped her hands. "I just wanted you to know."

She started to slip under his arm and move away, but he caught her. "No, you don't. You don't drop a bomb like that and walk off."

She stopped and looked up at him, her gaze as clear and honest as a baby's. Something dangerous turned over inside Collin's chest. She was serious. She loved him.

Oh, man. How did he deal with that? And why had she chosen to tell him now in the midst of a conversation about God and Drew?

If her intention was to distract him, she'd succeeded. The idea of kissing her had been on his mind since she'd bopped out of that yellow Mustang and sashayed across his front yard with her family in tow.

Ah, what was he talking about? He'd wanted to kiss her a lot longer than that.

Now that he knew she loved him, he wasn't quite so hesitant to follow through.

Drawing her closer, he lowered his face to hers.

She shrank back against the house and placed a hand on his chest. "I'm sorry, Collin. As much as I'd like to kiss you, I won't."

He frowned. "You love me? But you won't let me kiss you?"

Her eyes filled with tears, confusing him more. He'd made her cry, though he had no idea what he'd done. "I'm sorry. Let me explain."

Reluctantly, he dropped his hands and backed off. Everything in him wanted to hold her more than ever now.

The wind circled in between them. Mia shivered and hugged herself, and he had to fight to keep from taking her in his arms again.

"I could do that for you," he said with a half smile.

But they both knew he wouldn't push the issue.

She rubbed her hands up and down her arms, eyes focused on some distant point in the darkness. "Tonight, I understood something about you, Collin."

"Yeah?" He wished she'd tell him because right now he didn't understand much of anything.

"I realized that you don't know how to receive love. From God or anybody else. You've been hurt and rejected so much in your life that you think you're unlovable."

He didn't much like the idea of anyone poking around inside his head, and he liked it even less when someone thought they knew what made him tick. But he had to admit, there was validity to her words. Normally, he didn't listen to psycho-babble, but from Mia—well, Mia was different.

"Love is a gift, Collin, and unless a gift is given away, it has no value. You're valuable to me. I wanted you to understand that. I wanted to give that to you."

"Then why—?" He left the question hanging. She loved him, but she wouldn't kiss him?

He shoved his hands into his jacket pockets.

Her logic didn't make sense.

"Because as much as I love you, I love God more. And I trust Him to know what's best and right for me even when His rules hurt."

Her words were a splash of cold water in the face. One minute she declared her love and the next she shut him out. "And God says I'm not good enough for you?"

"That's not what I mean."

She closed the distance between them and rested her head against his chest. He didn't yield. He'd never let a woman get this close. And now she was telling him she loved him but he wasn't good enough?

But in his heart, he knew she was right. A foster kid from questionable bloodlines could never be good enough for a woman like Mia.

"Will you hear me out?" she asked softly. "This has nothing to do with being good enough."

He relented then, letting her tug one hand from his pocket. He couldn't seem to say no to Mia.

"You have a lot of baggage from the past to deal with, Collin. None of that scares me off. God can heal anything. But that's the key. You have to let Him."

"What does any of that have to do with me kissing you? Does God have rules against a man kissing a woman he cares about?"

Okay, so he cared about her. Maybe a lot, though love wasn't a word in his vocabulary.

Mia's full mouth widened in a characteristic smile. "God's all for kissing. He probably invented it. But he has rules about Christians kissing non-Christians. That's hard for me to accept, but I have to. I'll be your friend. And I won't stop loving you even for a second, but that's as far as we go."

"You mean if I was a Christian, I could kiss you?"

"Yes." She tilted her head to one side and gave him a lopsided smile. "But don't be thinking I go around kissing just anybody, Christian or not."

He already knew that about her.

"Okay, then. Friends. I can do that." Friendship was all he'd ever expected anyway. Just knowing she was in love with him was burden enough.

Yes, friendship was far better anyway.

Mia dropped the last gaily wrapped gift into her shopping bag and headed out of the mall. The Christmas crowd was thicker than Grandma Carano's spaghetti sauce.

She had met her best girlfriend for a late lunch and they'd talked about Collin. Sharing her concerns with a praying friend had helped. She was thinking about her cop far too much lately and though convinced she'd done the right thing by admitting her love for him, holding to the friendship rule was harder than she'd imagined.

Collin had the uncanny ability to move right on as if nothing had happened. But with a subtle difference. Last night, he'd come to her apartment, bearing a glorious red poinsettia and asked her out to dinner. When she'd refused, he'd wanted to stay and talk about the book she'd loaned him.

Not knowing if she was playing with fire or trying to be a good witness for the Lord, she'd made microwave popcorn and spent the next two hours in an interesting discussion about her faith. Collin was a bright man with a lot of questions and misconceptions about God. He was stuck on the idea that God had abandoned him along with everyone else in his childhood, and nothing she said seemed to help.

But he was seeking the truth, and that alone was a big step.

Upon leaving the crowded mall, Mia picked Mitchell up from school and took him back to her office. They had some things to discuss that couldn't be said at his home. Later, she had his mother's permission to take him Christmas shopping with the money Collin had paid him for working with the animals. No matter that she'd already spent two hours at the mall, shopping was something Mia could always do.

Mitchell looked scruffy and smelled worse. She hoped the odor was normal boy sweat and not cigarette smoke. He'd come too far these six months to regress now.

Once inside her small office, she handed him a stick of beef jerky and motioned to a chair. "Sit down. We need to talk."

He ripped into the jerky. "About Collin?"

That surprised her. "Why do you think this is about Collin?"

One shoulder hitched. He flopped into the chair. "Since we didn't go out to his place, I figure something's up. He said I don't have to come anymore."

"You don't."

"I guess he's tired of me hanging around."

Mia rounded her desk and sat down. "You know

that's not true. Your official community service time is completed so nobody will force you to work on the farm anymore. Now the decision to go or not is yours to make."

"Did he and Adam find the guy who started the fire?"

"They think so."

He chewed thoughtfully, then spoke around a wad of jerky. "I don't."

Mia frowned. "What do you mean?"

Mitchell took a sudden interest in the tip of his beef stick. "Nothing."

"Is there something you want to tell me?"

He slouched a little lower in the chair. "No."

Which meant there was.

She sighed and let the subject drop. Mitchell shared confidences according to his timetable, not hers. "Collin needs your help now more than ever."

"It really stinks about his brother. I wish I could do something."

"You already do. You help with the animals. Keep him company. Cheer him up. He depends on you." The boy *was* good for Collin, and the cop was finally at a place where he could realize as much.

Mitchell sat up straighter. "Yeah. I guess he does. He hates mucking out stalls." One tennis-shoed foot banged the front of her desk. "But I meant about his brother."

"We can't do anything about Drew's death, Mitch."

"I meant the other one."

She smiled. "Sooner or later, we'll find Ian."

She let a couple of seconds pass. The subject she needed to broach wasn't a good one. Muffled voices came and went outside her closed door.

"You want a Coke?" she asked to soften him up.

"Nah."

"Later then. We'll go to that Mexican place you like."

"Cool." His toe tapped the front of her metal desk over and over again.

Mia picked up a pen. Put it down. Took it up again. "We need to discuss your stepdad."

Mitchell stiffened. The thudding against her desk ceased. He didn't look up.

"I know you're scared of him."

No answer.

"I talked to your mother about going to a women's shelter, but she refuses. She says there's nothing wrong. Frankly, I don't believe her, and I'm worried about both of you." When he didn't respond, she dropped the pen and leaned toward him. She was getting nowhere with this one-sided conversation.

"Mitch, if something should happen, anything at all, if you should ever be afraid, will you call me? Or Collin?"

He thought about her question for several seconds while a telephone rang in another office and a door down the hall slammed shut. Finally, he nodded. "Yeah."

That was the best she was going to get. She rubbed the back of her neck and stretched. "I'll trust you on that."

Her office door opened and another social worker peeked inside. "Mia, could I see you for a minute?"

"Of course." She stood and said to Mitch, "Stay put, okay?" She glanced at the clock. "When I get back we'll head for the mall."

"Can I play on your computer?"

"Sure. And have another beef jerky. I'll be back in a few minutes."

Three days later, Collin bounded up the stairs to the second floor of the Department of Human Services. Mia had said she loved him, but he'd never believed she'd do this.

She looked up from a stack of paperwork, the kind of overwhelming mountain he understood too well. Jammed into one corner of her office, a miniature Christmas tree blinked multi-colored lights. A whimsical Santa waved from the wall behind her desk, and Christmas carols issued from her computer speakers.

"Oh, hi, Collin." Mia's face lit up. "I got your note."

"Sorry I missed you." More than sorry. Every day since she'd said those shocking words he'd found an excuse to talk to her, either in person or on the phone.

The last couple of days she'd been out of contact and he'd missed her. He'd wanted to surprise her with a special offer that was sure to make her happy. Instead, she'd surprised him.

Somehow the knowledge that she loved him had changed him. He wasn't sure what was happening inside him, but he liked the difference. He felt lighter, happier, freer, which made no sense at all considering the news of Drew's death.

But then today in his mailbox… He slapped the brown envelope down onto her desk. He could never repay her for this.

"This is the best news I've had in a long time."

She grinned at his unusual enthusiasm. "You could use some good news."

He didn't want to think she'd done this out of pity, but if he told the truth, he didn't really care why she'd done it.

"I think this is Ian, don't you?"

She blinked, puzzled. "Excuse me?"

He slid a sheet of paper from the envelope and laid the all-important document in front of her. "I think this is my Ian. I think this is the agency that handled his adoption."

And he hadn't even known Ian was adopted. Part of him rejoiced. At least one brother had found a family.

"Collin, I don't know what you're talking about—" She froze in midsentence as her eyes moved across the confidential document.

All the color drained from her face. Disbelief mixed with hurt, she shot to her feet. Rollers clattered as her chair thunked against the wall behind her. "I can't believe this, Collin. How could you?"

Now he was confused. "How could I what?"

"Break into these confidential files. Compromise me this way. I thought we were at least friends."

They were friends. A lot more than friends. "What are you talking about?"

"You were here in my office while I was gone."

He rocked back, stunned at the unspoken accusation. "You think I broke into your files?"

"What else can I think? This document is from a sealed adoption file. No one, not even me, is supposed to look at those files without express permission or a court order."

He knew how important her professional integrity was. He'd never even considered such a thing. "I wouldn't do that."

"Somebody did."

His jaw grew hard enough to bite through concrete as her accusation hit home. "And you think it was me."

She stared at the twinkling Christmas tree. He sensed a battle going on behind those warm gray-green eyes, but her silence was an affirmation. Finally she said, "Who else would want to?"

He had an idea but if she couldn't figure that one out on her own, he wasn't about to toss out accusations. Not like she'd done. "You'll have to trust me on this, Mia."

She pushed the sheet of paper back into the envelope and handed the packet across the desk. Her hands trembled. "I hope you find him."

"Will you help me?" He needed her. And he wanted her there beside him when Ian was found.

She shook her head, expression bleak. "I'm sorry, Collin. I can't."

She didn't believe him.

All his joy shriveled into a dusty wad. He'd finally let a woman into his heart and she couldn't even give him her trust. Some love that was.

Fine. Dandy. He should have known.

He yanked the envelope from the desk and stalked out.

Mia locked the door of her office and cried. From her computer radio, Karen Carpenter's lush voice sang "Merry Christmas Darling." She clicked Mute.

How could Collin have done such a thing? He'd been in here two days ago, at her desk while she was at lunch. He'd even left a note. She'd wanted to believe he wouldn't do this to her, but how could she? Hadn't he pressured her more than once to open those files?

Over and over she remembered when Gabe had badgered confidential information from her. Just like Collin he'd said, "Trust me, Mia. You know I wouldn't do anything that could hurt you."

But in the end, her actions on his behalf had hurt

her plenty. She'd lost her job and her credibility. And though Gabe had worked hard to make the loss up to her, she couldn't forget the awful sense of betrayal and shame.

Her own flesh-and-blood brother had compromised her for his own gain. How could she believe that Collin wouldn't do the same for a much more worthwhile reason?

Not that she wasn't glad he had the information about Ian. She only wished he'd come by it more honestly.

Collin stewed for two days, hammering away his anger on the barn that didn't seem to be getting any larger.

He hadn't broken into Mia's computer, but even if he had, he wouldn't lie about it. Why couldn't she see that? He'd considered questioning Mitch, but why bother? The deed was done and Mia blamed him.

If he'd known falling for a Christian was this much trouble, he would have run even harder the day she'd bought him a hamburger.

His cell phone rang and he slapped the device from his belt loop. "Grace."

"Mr. Grace, this is the Loving Homes Adoption Agency in Baton Rouge. I think I may have some information for you."

His heart slammed against his ribcage. His hammer dropped to the ground. Happy gazed up at him, puzzled as he grappled in his shirt pocket for a pencil. With shaking fingers, he scribbled the information on a piece of plywood.

His brother's name might be Ian Carpenter.

Everything in him wanted to call Mia, to share the excitement of finally having a concrete lead.

But he wouldn't. She wouldn't want him to.

# *Chapter Fourteen*

The call came in at ten minutes to nine in the morning. A hostage situation. The suspect a convicted felon, armed and dangerous. And probably high on drugs.

Collin donned his gear along with the rest of the Tac-team members as the captain drilled them on the situation. During the serving of a warrant, the suspect had gone ballistic and taken a woman hostage, probably the common-law wife.

Collin exchanged glances with Maurice. He knew his buddy was already praying and he was glad. In situations like this, they needed all the help they could get. The Christmas holidays were high-stress periods. If anyone was going off the deep end, this time of year seemed to bring it on.

As the van approached the neighborhood, Collin grew uneasy. He knew this area.

"This is the Perez house," he said.

Captain Gonzales nodded. "Isn't that the name of the kid you've been mentoring?"

"Yeah. Is he in there?"

"Not anymore. We just got a call from Shipley on somebody's cell phone. There's a social worker inside with him. Not the wife."

Collin's blood ran cold. "Who's the social worker?"

He already knew before the captain spoke. "Adam Carano's sister, Mia. You know her?"

He and Maurice exchanged quick glances.

"We've met." What was Mia doing in there? Hadn't he told her to stay away?

The captain gave him a strange look. He'd told no one except Maurice about his friendship with Mia. If the captain knew he was personally involved he'd send him back to the station. No way Collin was going to leave Mia at the mercy of some doped-up maniac whose last address was the state penitentiary.

Keeping his face passive, he readied his equipment, mind racing with the possibilities. Anything could go down in a situation like this. Anything.

"Why's the social worker involved? Was she there to grab the kid?"

"Bad timing, I think. She was inside when an arrest warrant was served. Shipley flipped out when he saw the cops approaching, and took her hostage."

Dandy.

"Anyone else in the house?"

"We don't know that yet either. Jeff is working on getting the floor plans from the rental company that owns the house. Gomez is talking to neighbors to see what they know."

They set up a command post in the parking lot of an apartment complex across the street. Team members quietly dispersed around the property while uniformed officers blocked off the streets and cleared the surrounding area of bystanders.

Collin climbed to the second floor of the apartment building, seeking an advantageous position from which to view the Perez place. Adrenaline raced through his bloodstream at a far greater rate than usual in a call-out. He'd practiced this scenario a thousand times. Had even executed it. But no one he loved had ever been inside the premises.

He squeezed his eyes shut and rubbed a hand over his forehead. Of all the times to realize he was in love, he'd sure picked a doozy.

Through the earpiece in his helmet he heard the captain. They'd made contact with Teddy Shipley. The guy was spewing all kinds of irrationalities, blaming the cops for harassing him, for his inability to get a job, asking for money, a car, amnesty from prosecution.

For the next hour and a half, the negotiator tried to soothe the frenzied suspect. Collin wished like crazy he could hear the conversation but all his information was filtered through the commander. He could hear the other officers, and from his vantage point above the scene he watched the stealth movement of Tac members maneuvering closer to the house, hoping for a chance.

After a while, the suspect moved the hostage into the living room, though even through his scope, Collin could see only their shadowy forms. One of those shadows belonged to Mia. The other much larger form definitely brandished a weapon. And as much as Collin wanted to charge the place and take the guy out with his own hands, right now all he could do was wait.

By noon, the tension hung as thick as L.A. fog. Shipley grew angrier and more demanding by the minute.

Collin, jaw tight, spoke into his mouthpiece. "Has anyone talked to the hostage?"

The answer crackled back. "Yes. She sounded okay. Scared, but pretty calm under the circumstances. We gathered from her subtle answers that Shipley is popping pills on top of meth. He's seriously messed up."

No big surprise there. Collin ground his teeth. No surprise but a really big problem.

At one o'clock, food was brought in. No one bothered to eat it.

At two o'clock, the negotiator still had not established a rapport. The suspect was spewing vitriol with the frequency and strength of a geyser. He was sick of being harassed. He wasn't taking it anymore. He wasn't going back to the pen. And scariest of all, they'd never take him alive.

By three in the afternoon, hope for a peaceful resolution was fading. Shipley came to the dirty window, dragging Mia with him, a nine millimeter at her temple. Collin saw her expression through his scope. Saw the fear in her eyes, the bruises on her face. Hot fury ripped through him.

Collin knew the minute Shipley spotted an officer outside the house. Wild-eyed and crazed, he fired one shot through the picture window. Glass shattered. Shipley shoved Mia toward the opening, screaming threats.

They had an active shooter with a hostage. Things could go south fast. Real fast.

The question came through his earpiece, terse but strong. "Have you got a visual?"

"Yeah." For a man whose knees had turned to water, his voice sounded eerily calm.

He slid down onto his belly, the rough shingles scraping against his vest. He had a visual, but Mia was in the way.

"If you have the shot, take it."

The surge of adrenaline prickled his scalp. His mouth went dry. To his horror, his hands, renowned for their steadiness, began to shake.

In twelve years on the force, he'd never missed,

never been scared, not even when he took down a cop killer. But Mia had never been the hostage. Her bright-red Christmas sweater and frightened eyes were imprinted in his brain.

What if he hit the woman he loved more than his own life? What if the ice-water-in-his-veins sniper they called Amazing Grace missed?

The December temperature was in the thirties, but sweat broke out all over Collin.

He was the only person standing between Mia and the maniac, and he was terrified.

He couldn't do this. But there was no one else. The other sniper had no shot. Mia's life was in his hands—hands that wouldn't stop shaking.

He needed help. And there was only one place to get it.

Intent on the house, he was afraid to blink and too focused to move. Under the circumstances, he figured God would understand if his prayers weren't too formal. There was no time to close his eyes and bow his head.

"Help me, Lord. I can't handle this one. Steady me. Give me the perfect shot. For Mia."

Then as if God had actually heard him, the strangest thing happened. His hands and guts stopped trembling. The usual cool detachment settled over him. Only the feeling wasn't cool. It was warm, comforting. Something incredible had just happened to him, but he had no time to dwell on it.

"Thanks," he whispered. Later, he'd do a lot better.

His gaze flicked from the felon to Mia. Eyes wide, she stared outward toward the invisible cops. As if in slow motion, Collin saw her mouth move. For a second, he thought she was praying, too, but then through his scope, he read her lips.

"Do it."

She knew he was out here. She knew he was the sniper on duty. And she trusted him to take care of her. Mia trusted him.

And he wasn't about to let her down.

With exacting skill, he trained the sights on the suspect and waited for the precise moment. No muscle quivered. Not an eyelash blinked.

Suddenly, Mia slumped in a faint.

Collin pulled the trigger. The crack ripped the air, and the suspect crumpled.

In the next few milliseconds that seemed like hours, the Tac-team swarmed the house. Voices screamed in his earpiece.

"Suspect down. Suspect down."

Collin pushed up from the roof. A minute ago, he'd been deadly calm. Now his legs wobbled with such force he wasn't sure he could walk. Rifle in hand, he started down. He made it to the first-floor stairwell and collapsed, sliding down with his back against the hard, block wall.

He could have killed her. He could have hit Mia.

"I will never leave you nor forsake you."

The words entered his head unbidden and he knew they didn't come from him. He shoved one hand into his pocket and withdrew the little keychain.

"Thank you," he muttered. Keychain in his fisted hand, he pressed the little fish to his mouth, dropped his head to his elevated knees, and did something he hadn't done since he was ten years old.

He wept.

"I don't need an ambulance. I'm okay. Really." Mia struggled against the strong arms of too many paramedics and police officers who wanted her to get into the ambulance. There was only one cop she wanted to see and he was nowhere around.

"Humor us, Mia." Maurice Johnson's familiar face materialized from the crowd. "You're in shock."

Maybe she was in shock. Except for an overriding sense of relief, she felt numb.

A paramedic wrapped a blood pressure cuff around her arm. As she started to resist, her knees buckled. Maurice grabbed her slumping form and helped the paramedic lift her into the back of the ambulance.

"Where's Collin?" she asked. The bruise on her cheekbone started to throb and her head swam.

"Right here."

A tall, lean officer in SWAT uniform pushed through the crowd. His handsome face exhausted, he was the most wonderful thing she'd ever seen.

"Collin," she said, and heard the wobble in her

voice, felt the tears in her eyes. She dove out of the ambulance into the strongest arms imaginable. Collin wouldn't let her fall.

"I'm sorry. I was so wrong. I do trust you. I do." The tears came in earnest then.

"I know." His lips brushed her ear. "It's okay. Everything is okay now."

She searched his face and saw something new. A peace she hadn't seen before.

He was still strong and solid and every bit the confident police officer, but something about him had changed.

Later, she'd have to ask. Yes, later, she thought, as she snuggled against his chest and the world went dark.

Collin didn't bother to clean up. Still in uniform, he made one stop before heading to the hospital.

When he walked into the room, Mia was sitting in a hospital bed, chattering at mach speed to convince a young doctor to let her go home.

"Might as well say yes," Collin said.

The blond resident gave him a weary smile. "Persistent, is she?"

"Like a terrier. She'll yap until you give in."

"You sound like a man of experience."

Collin looked at the smiling Mia and his heart wrenched. Her pretty face was swollen and bruised from eye to chin. But that didn't keep her from talking.

"Just trust me on this." He winked at Mia. "And

let her go. She'll be well taken care of. I can promise you that."

The doctor scribbled something on the chart and dropped the clipboard into a slot at the foot of the bed. "I'll see what I can do."

As he left, Collin scraped a heavy green chair up to the bedside. "How ya doin'?"

"Better. How are you?"

No one had ever asked him that before except the force psychologist.

"It's part of the job."

"I didn't ask you that." She took the single red rose from him and pressed the bud to her nose. "I knew you were out there today. And I knew you and God would take care of me."

"How?"

She tapped her heart. "I felt you. In here. Just the way I felt God's presence. You saved my life."

Just thinking about what could have happened made Collin want to crush her to him and never let her go. "I've never been that scared."

"You?"

"Terrified," he admitted. "I prayed, Mia. And the strangest thing happened. My hands were shaking and I couldn't do my job. One prayer later, I'm a changed man."

"Oh, Collin." Hope flared in her sweet eyes.

He smiled, the tenderness inside him a scary thing.

He had to tell her. He had to say the words no matter how difficult. With Mia, he could be vulnerable.

"I realized that I need God in my life even more than I need you. And I need you more than my next breath. I love you, Mia. Please say you haven't given up on me."

Collin had never seen an angel, but he couldn't imagine anything more beautiful than the expression on Mia's face.

"I don't ever give up, Collin. Don't you know that by now?" She shifted on the bed, grimaced at the IV in her arm. "Mitchell came by with another social worker. He wanted to tell me not to be mad at you anymore."

"He broke into your confidential files?"

"How did you guess?"

"I figured as much all along."

"And said nothing."

"Now don't get your back up. I wanted him to be man enough to own up to mistakes on his own."

"He told us something else, too. Shipley set your barn on fire. Revenge for messing in his business, as he put it. He's just a mean man."

Now that was a stunner. "I guess I owe my neighbor an apology on that at least."

"What about the lawsuit?"

"You brother convinced Mr. Slokum to play nice. He dropped the case when Adam brought up the half brother."

"Adam's a good lawyer."

"What's going to happen to Mitch now?" He hated to ask the obvious. "Foster care?"

She offered a smug smile. "Yes, but I have a plan."

"Which means someone is about to be hit by a bulldozer named Mia."

"The people I have in mind are used to it."

"If you're thinking who I'm thinking, I approve."

"Mom and Dad love him. He's crazy about them. They're starting the paperwork and foster-care classes, but I think I can pull a few strings so he can live with them now while his mom is in treatment."

"Miss Carano, I love you. Even if you are a social worker."

With a relieved and happy heart, he leaned across the metal rail and kissed her. When she didn't protest, he kissed her again. This time she kissed him back.

# Epilogue

The halls were decked with tinsel and garland and rows and rows of white lights. Christmas carols played softly, and the stockings really were hung by the chimney with care.

The Carano Christmas was in full swing. Mia had managed to spirit Collin away from the prying eyes and teasing brothers to give him her gift in private.

"Open your present."

"I don't need presents. I have you, your awesome family and an even more awesome relationship with Christ. What more could a man want?"

He was different since accepting the Lord into his life. Not that his quiet personality had changed, but he was less tense, warmer, freer.

She pressed a small box, wrapped in shiny blue paper and topped with silver ribbon, into his hands. "Don't argue with me, mister. You know I'll win."

Mia watched him, her heart in her throat. He took his time sliding the ribbon over the corners. Turning the box over and over, he slowly caressed the slick, smooth foil with his fingertips.

Mia bubbled with impatience, but she didn't interfere. He grinned up at her. "I haven't done this many times. Let me enjoy the moment."

The notion that his Christmases weren't filled with good memories stabbed at her. She was determined to make up for lost time, and her family felt the same. They'd finally managed to draw him into the fold and he had begun giving back the banter, though his was still far more reserved than Nic's or Adam's.

Finally, when Mia thought she'd have to rip the gift from his hands and open the box herself, he pulled away the last bit of tape. Tissue paper crinkled as he lifted out the blue-and-white Christmas ornament.

The fragile bulb, held gently in his palm, glimmered beneath the bright light. The old black-and-white photo of three small boys was perfectly centered amidst a snowy Christmas scene. Collin, Drew and Ian in a photo she'd found stuck in a file.

"How did you—?"

The expression on his face was one she would never forget. The cop who hid his feelings couldn't hide them now.

Awe. Yearning. Joy.

With exquisite care, he replaced the bulb and set the box aside to wrap his arms around Mia.

She knew him. Knew he would struggle with the right words to express his feelings. His heart thundered against her ear. She heard him swallow once. Twice.

"I knew you'd love it."

"Yeah." His chest rose and fell as he continued to press back a tide of emotion. This was one of the things she'd learned to love the most about him. He was so deeply emotional. He felt things so intensely, but all his life he'd stuffed them deeper to avoid hurt.

Finally, he sighed and then with the same sweet tenderness kissed the top of her head. "It's the best present I've ever had."

"Want to hang it on the tree?"

He cast a sideways glance toward the noisy living room. "Dare we go back in there?"

"Actually, I'd rather stay right here with you forever."

"But your brothers would never allow that to happen."

As if on cue, Adam's voice yelled down the hallway. "What's taking you two so long? We got a party going on in here."

"Yeah," Nic hollered. "And I wanna open my presents."

Mia giggled and took Collin's hand. "Be brave."

Such a silly thing to say to a man who had never been anything else in his entire life.

As they entered the living room, everyone

quieted. Mitchell stood by the enormous Christmas tree with Nic, Adam and Gabe. Each male wore a Cheshire grin.

"Now you've corrupted Mitchell," she said to them. "What are you up to?"

They all looked at Collin. He, in turn, flicked at glance at her dad who gave a slight nod. Her mother and grandmother, each holding one of Gabe's kids, beamed from the couch. Her very pregnant sister, Anna Maria, waddled across the room and handed Collin a beautiful maroon velvet box topped with a gold plaid bow.

He cleared his throat. "Your present," he said.

Mia got a fluttery feeling in the pit of her stomach. Her gaze ran around the room, saw the intense, excited faces of all the people who loved her best. Gabe aimed the video camera in her direction.

They knew something she didn't.

She lifted the lid and frowned in puzzlement. Lavender rose petals sprang out of the box and fluttered to the floor. She plunged her hands into the velvety petals, releasing the rich spicy scent as she pulled out yet another box. A velvet jeweler's box.

She gasped and looked up at Collin, her mouth open in surprise.

"Look guys," Nic muttered. "Mia's speechless."

She was too stunned and thrilled to react to the titter of amusement circling the warm, festive room.

"Mia." Collin took the final box from her shaking

fingers and went down on one knee in front of her. "I'm not too good with words." He cleared his throat again.

One of the brothers guffawed. Collin slanted him a look. "Give me a break, Nic."

"Want me to ask her for you?"

"Shut up, Adam," Mia said good-naturedly. She touched a trembling palm to Collin's cheek. "You were saying?"

"I love you."

"I love you, too."

"All my life I've distrusted other people. I've kept them on the outside. But you wouldn't let me do that. You forced me to open up, to feel. And I'm so glad you did. To love and know that I'm loved back is an awesome thing."

Mia's heart was about to burst with love. She knew how hard this was for him. For a man of few words, he'd just said a mouthful.

In the background came the soft strains of "I'll Be Home for Christmas."

"Mia." A quiver ran from Collin's hand into hers. He bent his head and placed a whisper of a kiss upon her hand, then slid the ring onto her finger. "Will you marry me?"

Tears sprang into her eyes.

"Yes, I will," was all she could manage as she collapsed against him. Sure and strong, he absorbed the impact and rocked her back and forth, laughing and laughing while she sobbed into his shoulder.

* * *

Much later, after Mia's brothers and dad had pounded his back in congratulations and the ladies had kissed his cheek declaring this the most romantic proposal they'd ever witnessed, Collin finally stopped shaking. He'd known how important Mia's family was to her and proposing this way would make her happy. He just hadn't known how nervous he'd be.

Then as if to overwhelm him to the point of no return, Mia's brothers had pledged their time and talents along with that of their church—now his church, too—to help rebuild and expand his animal rehab facility. Their Christmas gift to him and the animals, they'd said. And he was too moved to speak.

"Spiced cider, anyone?" Rosalie manned the large urn that emitted the rich scents of cinnamon and apple.

Standing with his back against the cold patio doors, his new fiancée leaning into him, the fragrance of her perfume embracing him, Collin felt more content than he could remember. He didn't need or want anything else.

Well, perhaps one other thing. "Could I tell you something?" he murmured against Mia's hair.

"Anything." She twisted around to smile at him and he couldn't resist another kiss.

"I followed up on that information Mitchell found."

She was quiet for a moment and he hoped he hadn't rekindled her anger over the unfortunate incident. "I'm glad."

"You are?"

"God turned Mitchell's mistake into something good. How could I be upset about that?"

He should have known she'd say that. "I have a phone number and a name. Someone who may be Ian."

She whirled around, sliding her arms around his waist, her expression joyous. "Collin, that's wonderful! Have you called? What did he say? When are you going to meet him?"

He swallowed a laugh. "Whoa, Miss Bulldog. I have the name and number but I haven't called yet."

"Why not?" But being Mia, she answered her own question. "You're nervous."

"Scared spitless. What if it isn't him?"

"What if it is?" She grabbed his arms and shook him a little. "Collin, you may have found Ian. Come on. Let's call right now. Where is that number?"

He took the slip of paper from his shirt pocket and shared the bits of information. "Ian Carpenter. The dates match. The age matches. I think it's him, but I've had hope before."

"This time, my love, you have something else. You have a family who will always love you and stand with you no matter what. And best of all you have the Lord. He'll—"

"Never leave me nor forsake me," Collin finished with a smile, feeling the truth of her words. He was full to the brim with the kind of love he'd craved all his life. Finding Ian would be icing on his very sweet cake.

He reached into his pocket and took out the small fish keychain, now polished to a pewter gleam.

Mia smiled gently, her face full of love, and stretched out a palm. Instead of handing her the keychain, he took her hand. "I love you, Mia."

"I love you, Collin."

"Good." He drew in a breath, feeling the strength of his faith urging him on. "Let's go make that call."

* * * * *

*Don't miss Ian Carpenter's story when*
THE BROTHERS' BOND
*continues in March 2007 with*
*A TOUCH OF GRACE,*
*only from Steeple Hill Love Inspired.*

Dear Reader,

In my other career, I'm an elementary school teacher. Some years ago my principal asked me to remain in the hallway after school for a few minutes. Social Services was on the way to pick up three of our students. My job was to meet the caseworker and direct her to the office. As long as I live, I will remember the scene inside that room. The three children, one stoic and accepting, one furious and fighting, and the last one silently crying, are imprinted on my memory forever. I've never been able to forget them. I've often wondered what happened to them, where they are now. They haunted me until the only way I could find closure was to create a story for each one, and of course, to give them the happy endings every child deserves.

I'm so pleased to bring this heartfelt new series, *The Brothers' Bond,* to you. I hope you fall in love with each one of "my boys," beginning this month with Collin.

I love hearing from readers. Please visit my Web site at www.lindagoodnight.com or send an e-mail to linda@lindagoodnight.com.

Blessings to you and yours this Christmas,

Linda Goodnight

## QUESTIONS FOR DISCUSSION

1. Mia and Collin are opposites in many ways, and yet they are the perfect complement for each other. Explore the elements of their personalities that make this true. What needs in Collin does Mia fill? What needs in Mia does Collin fill?
2. The saying goes "The child is father to the man." How does this apply to Collin?
3. Which do you think has the biggest effect on a person's character, environment or heredity? Can you find examples in the story to support your answer?
4. Collin is reluctant to get involved as Mitchell's Big Brother. Why? What do his lost brothers have to do with this reluctance?
5. Mia considers her job as a social worker to be a calling. What is a calling? Do you believe someone outside the ministry can be called by God? Has He placed a calling on your life? How can one know for certain if they are called by God?
6. The American foster-care system has come under scrutiny because of kids like Collin who age out without ever having found a family. Is foster care the solution for kids from deeply troubled homes? Is there a better solution?

7. Collin has never had anyone but himself to rely on. How does this affect his coming to Christ? At what point in the book does he realize that he can no longer rely only on himself?

8. Mia refuses to get romantically involved with Collin even after she falls in love with him. Do you think it's important for a Christian to date only Christians? Does it really matter? Why or why not? Discuss the pros and cons.

9. For years, Collin has carried the Christian fish symbol engraved with the words "Jesus will never leave you nor forsake you." Do you believe this is true? Have you ever experienced a time when you felt abandoned by the Lord? What did you do?

10. Mia tells Collin that *grace* means unmerited favor. What does God's grace mean to you? How have you experienced grace in your life, both from God and from another person?